W9-COD-515

A DANGEROUS DANCE

There were rattlesnakes everywhere, writhing and striking out waspishly, and, in a pandemonium of yells and curses, Lady Grace's soldier guard broke and fled. From his vantage ground on the roof Lord Benedict was working madly to photograph this last wild scene, and, while his daughter stood beside him to hand him his plate holder, he ducked under his black focusing cloth. For a moment he racked the lens back and forth, and, when he came out, she was gone. Only the plate holder, halfway to the hatchway, marked the direction in which she had vanished.

Other *Leisure* books by Dane Coolidge:

BITTER CREEK
THE WILD BUNCH
MAN FROM WYOMING

SNAKE DANCE

DANE COOLIDGE

LEISURE BOOKS NEW YORK CITY

A LEISURE BOOK®

February 2007

Published by special arrangement with Golden West Literary Agency.

Dorchester Publishing Co., Inc.
200 Madison Avenue
New York, NY 10016

If you purchased this book without a cover you should be aware that this book is stolen property. It was reported as "unsold and destroyed" to the publisher and neither the author nor the publisher has received any payment for this "stripped book."

Copyright © 2005 by Golden West Literary Agency

All rights reserved. No part of this book may be reproduced or transmitted in any form or by any electronic or mechanical means, including photocopying, recording or by any information storage and retrieval system, without the written permission of the publisher, except where permitted by law.

ISBN 0-8439-5811-1

The name "Leisure Books" and the stylized "L" with design are trademarks of Dorchester Publishing Co., Inc.

Printed in the United States of America.

Visit us on the web at www.dorchesterpub.com.

EDITOR'S NOTE

The text of this story was taken from the second-draft typescript with holographic and typed corrections and additions made by Dane Coolidge and dated by him as having been completed during October and November, 1930. Each section, as it was completed, was separately dated in the author's hand, beginning October 8, 1930. The second-draft corrected typescript differs significantly from the three outlines of the story that Coolidge wrote earlier in 1930 as well as the first draft, completed in August. The author's original title was *Lady Grace's Crossing*. For publication this title has been changed to an alternative suggested by the author. Acknowledgment is made to Mary A. Whittier, trustee of the Estate of Dane Coolidge, for having supplied all versions and drafts of this story.

CHAPTER ONE

It was ration day at old Fort Defiance and within the shadow of the blood-red cliff the whole Navajo tribe was gathered. There were warriors newly conquered but still proud of their battles, gorgeous in striped blankets, heavily hung with turquoise, the spoils of the oft-raided Hopis. They paused as they passed the broad headquarters verandah where Major Doyle entertained his new guests, shaking hands with Lord Benedict as if they did him honor, glancing briefly at his daughter, Lady Grace.

From beyond the Eastern Ocean these two strangers had come, crossing the plains alone in a wagon that gleamed like gold or the strands of Slender Woman's hair. Estsan Tsosi they had named her, and every move that she made was followed by admiring eyes. Never before among the white people had they seen a woman so fair—so slender and supple, so glad-eyed and friendly, so gifted with the beauty of the sun. When she spoke, they listened to the music of her voice as if the Talking God, who ascends to heaven with the dawn, had broken his long, forbidding silence. But they did not gawk and stare, like the Hopi boy who stood by the gate.

With them it was all a great wonder, to see how this girl from beyond the seas made every man do her will. Even Iron Tooth, as the Indians referred to the grim Major Doyle, who ruled them with his soldiers, had learned to respond with a smile. On the wide parade grounds, to please her soldier father, a troop of cavalry flashed their sabers in the sun, while, stripped down and painted for war, the Navajo scouts went through a sham battle— for her. It was to show how Chief Manuelito and his two warrior brothers had taken their enemies alive.

Charging against their ranks, Manuelito crossed lances with the opposing chief and broke through. Closely behind, his huge brother snatched the chief as he dodged and jerked him out of the saddle. The third brother also followed closely to cover their retreat, and they bore the struggling victim away. Then in a cloud of dust the triumphant scouts whirled and raced their tough ponies back, but Silver Hat, the free scout, was far in the lead and Lady Grace clasped her hands in ecstasy.

"Oh, Father!" she exclaimed, "we *must* get his picture! Just look at that great hat with the silver eagle on it! Don't you think he would pose for us, Major?"

Major Doyle, the iron-toothed Indian fighter, looked down at her with eyes so deeply set that they seemed like holes burned in a blanket. His rawhide back, drawn straight as a whiplash, relaxed to easier lines, his curved nostrils seemed less eager for the fray. All his manhood had been spent among the warriors of the plains until now; he was cast in their mold, but with her he flashed his gold tooth in a smile.

"If *you* ask him," he said.

Counting the deed done, his lordship set up his camera. First he planted the heavy tripod, while the Indians gathered to look. But when he screwed on the black box, with its long bellows and staring glass eye, they covered their faces with their robes and stepped back. All except the lone Hopi who stood by the gate, in the midst of his ancient enemies. He pressed closer, smiling disdainfully at their fears while Lord Benedict draped the lens with his black cloth.

The scouts circled back, their bronze bodies gleaming, heavy buckskins belted tightly about their vitals to protect them from enemy arrows. But Silver Hat wore a beaded shirt. Beneath his broad hat his black hair hung to his shoulders, his swarthy face as dark as the rest. From leggings to red moccasins, he was an Indian of the Indians, but his laughing eyes were blue. Not until she stepped close to ask for his picture did Lady Grace perceive their hue, and she hesitated and forgot her sign talk.

"Does he speak English?" she stammered, glancing back at the grinning major. "I . . . er . . . want your picture. With me!"

She smiled enticingly, holding out a slender hand that seemed as white as the snows, but the tall scout did not stir. His face had frozen and from that grim Indian mask the blue eyes stared straight ahead.

"Oh, *you* ask him!" she appealed in a panic, and the major strode down the steps.

"Silver Hat," he said, "this is Lady Grace Benedict. She wants her picture taken, standing with you, to show to her friends in England."

Every eye among the scouts was fixed on Silver Hat, for they knew what Slender Woman desired, and he turned to Desteen, the old medicine man. They spoke together in Navajo—a young warrior joined in. Then Silver Hat shook his head and said: "No."

"Oh, please!" she cried reproachfully, and in the silence that followed the young Hopi edged up closer.

"They think it's bad luck to have their pictures taken," explained the major. "And especially with a woman."

"But he isn't an Indian," she protested. "I can tell by the color of his eyes."

"No, but he was raised among them, and as a rule they object to being photographed. They believe that some enemy, if he gets hold of the picture, can make war medicine over it and kill them."

"And do you believe that?" she demanded of Silver Hat. When he nodded, the Indians grunted approval.

Lady Grace stepped back, unbelieving and resentful, and into her dark brown eyes beneath the wind-whipped golden hair there came an angry gleam.

"*I* am not afraid," said a voice at her elbow, and she turned to see the smiling Hopi. He was naked except for a breechclout and moccasins and the yellow handkerchief that bound back his hair, but he was confident and at his ease.

"Who are you?" she asked, looking him over, and Major Doyle growled impatiently.

"I am Harold Polinuivah of the Hopis, or Peace People," he replied in perfect English. "Other Indians are afraid to speak their own name, but I have been to school. You can have your picture taken with me."

He held out his arm, and after one glance into his lustrous eyes, Lady Grace felt an instinct to obey. There was something in their depths that moved her against her will, something disarming and at the same time compelling, and never before in her trip across the plains had she seen a more handsome young savage. Every muscle stood out when he moved and he carried his tousled head gallantly. But there was a look in his dark eyes that roused uneasy fears, a dusky shadow beneath the heavy lashes, a hidden, blue-black gleam that clutched at her heart.

"Stand away, sir!" commanded her father, emerging wrathfully from beneath his black cloth, but Lady Grace had recovered her poise. She glanced back at Silver Hat and the scowling scouts who had denied her simple request and with a gracious smile placed her hand on Harold's arm and turned to face the camera.

"Now, take the picture, *Pater*," she said. "It will be wonderful for our book."

She stood waiting expectantly, vaguely conscious of the smoke smell that emanated, along with others, from her escort, but her father, fussing angrily with his focusing cloth and plate holders, was making slow work of it all. At last he held up his hand and removed the black cap that hooded the magic eye, but Harold Polinuivah did not quail. One, two, three, while the seconds were counted off, he stood braced against the invisible blow, and, when the picture was taken and Lady Grace had dashed away, he followed her to the porch.

"If you are writing a book," he said, "I can show you a great scene. Never has been witnessed before. I come from Yahoya, in Kahwestimah, where Snake Dance is given this month. My father is Masawa, the snake priest. They hold rattlesnakes in their mouths. You come . . . I show it all."

"What's this?" demanded the major, dismissing his scouts with a nod and looking down his nose at the Hopi. "I thought I told you to go home!"

"It must be wonderful . . . ," sighed Lady Grace.

The major cut her short: "That country north of the river is not safe," he said, and bustled her into the house. "Keep away from that Hopi," he advised, slamming the door.

Lady Grace burst out laughing. "Why, Major," she chided, "aren't the Hopis called the Peace People? Then what harm could possibly come if we visited their village and witnessed this curious Snake Dance?"

"That boy and his father," burst out Doyle, "make me more trouble than all the Apaches. They are the last Irreconcilables, the old, devil-worshipping Hopis, resisting the government to the end. When we march to Red Mesa, they meet us at the ladder and beg us to cut their heads off. They thrust out their necks and beg us to strike them dead. By the gods, I only wish they'd fight."

"What's that?" inquired Lord Benedict, hurrying in with his camera. "You say the country is dangerous? I was really quite taken with what the cheeky beggar said . . . would he allow me to photograph this Snake Dance?"

"All this country is dangerous," pronounced the major grimly. "We're patrolling the emigrant trail every day. Not a week passes but that some wagon is cut off. North of the Rio Bravo, where these Hopis live, I cannot guarantee your safety."

"Why, I was given to understand that the Hopis were peaceful. What was that about baring their breasts? I'd jolly well like to witness this Snake Dance, where they hold poisonous reptiles in their mouths."

"Not in Kahwestimah!" replied the major with finality. "If you want to visit the Navajos, I'll give you an escort anywhere. But old Masawa and his snake clan are dangerous."

"In what way, may I ask?" inquired his lordship, "since you say they are non-resistants?"

"If you must know," burst out Doyle, "we suspect them of stealing women. Several captives have been taken from emigrant trains and traced into this Kahwestimah country. They have never been heard from since."

Colonel Benedict sat bolt upright and stared at Major Doyle, who met his gaze with outthrust jaw. "My dear," suggested his lordship to his daughter, "will you retire to your room for a moment? I must get to the bottom of this."

"Yes, Father," she responded dutifully, and the two men were left alone.

"Now, Major," began the Englishman, "I am your guest. And at the same time, in a way, I am your charge, since I have brought letters from the State Department through the British Embassy at Washington. I should very much like to visit this strange country called Kahwestimah, but, if conditions render the journey really dangerous, we shall be obliged, of course, to forego it. What's this about stealing women?"

"Last spring," confided the major, leaning closer and glancing uneasily at the door, "an emigrant train was attacked, five hundred miles east of here, and Missus Adams and her two daughters taken prisoners. Her husband and their Negro servant were out gathering wood and escaped. All the rest of the small party were killed. Several days later a detachment of cavalry took up the trail and followed it north, but in the mountains above Taos the Indians separated and lost themselves among the rocks. Only one track was found, and it was followed to Yahoya, on the Red Mesa. I ordered out my scouts and we searched the country for hundreds of miles. Yellow hair had been found in the camps along the trail and fragments of women's clothes. The government offered a reward of a thousand dollars apiece for the return of these three captives, but they were never seen again. I am satisfied they were hidden and then killed."

"Yes, yes." Lord Benedict nodded. "I quite understand, having encountered similar cases myself. As a young man I was stationed with Her Majesty's troops in the mountains of northern Burma . . . but of that another time. What I wish to inquire is . . . why do you suspect this young Hopi? Was he connected in any way with the raid?"

"Not that we know of," admitted the major grudgingly, "but we found Hopi arrows in the bodies. That shows that they made the attack. It is other things, since, that have drawn my attention to this smooth-talking Harold Polinuivah. The biggest mistake the government ever made was when they rounded up these stiff-necked Hopis and put their children in school. His father resisted and we took them by force, and put old Masawa in the military prison. He stayed there three years and came back worse than ever . . .

still begging us to cut off his head. It seems they have some prophecy of the white man's coming, and that the first time we cut a Hopi's head off our race will be swept from the earth. That's why the damned rascals are always holding out their necks . . . they really want us to kill them."

"I see," observed Lord Benedict. "But about this boy, Harold? He seems a very presentable young chap, though I must say he presumes rather far. But with such a native to guide us through the country . . . ?"

"No, sir," rapped out the major, "not while you are under my protection. You don't understand, Lord Benedict, the conditions that prevail. Even along the trail, which is patrolled by my soldiers, we have had three raids in one month. The Apaches from here west are always watching for stragglers, but I've come to suspect that these Peace People from Kahwestimah are at the bottom of all this trouble. To tell you the truth, I believe Harold Polinuivah is sent here to spy on the wagon trains."

"Perhaps so," responded his lordship stiffly. "But with all due respect I must beg to differ with you regarding the conditions on the trail. My daughter and I have traveled without suffering the slightest inconvenience. We have found the Indians in all cases our friends, and certainly a noble type of savage. They have received us into their teepees and their curious mud houses with the greatest deference and respect, and my daughter, if I may say so, has won every heart. They have treated her like a goddess."

"Those Indians have been tamed by United States soldiers," returned the major, throwing back his head. "But from here west the country is different. Among the Navajos you are safe, but the Apaches are plain murderers. They don't take women captives . . . they kill them. So keep with your train . . . if you please."

"Is that an order?" inquired Lord Benedict, raising his eyebrows.

"It's a request," stated Major Doyle.

"Very well." The Englishman nodded. "As your guest I must accede. But it seems a pity, after coming so far, to be turned back by your fear of these natives. I am an old campaigner myself, Major Doyle, having served Her Majesty in both India and Egypt, and not without honor and wounds. But in my humble judgment this fear of a nonresistant Peace People is the veriest piffle and rot."

"It may seem so," returned the major meaningfully, "but I haven't told you it all. As soon as I saw this Harold Polinuivah, I knew he had designs on your daughter. There is some mysterious reason, perhaps connected with their religion, behind this abducting of women. Missus Adams and her daughters, all three, had yellow hair. You will excuse me if I mention that Lady Grace also . . ."

"Impossible!" cried Lord Benedict, starting up.

He strode over to her door and tapped on it lightly, frowned impatiently, and rapped again.

"She's not there," he announced, peering in, and Major Doyle leaped to his feet.

"I knew it," he muttered, snatching open the front door. There on the broad verandah sat Lady Grace herself, conversing with Harold Polinuivah.

CHAPTER TWO

"Father, dear," began Lady Grace, as the white-faced men came out, "I've discovered something wonderful for our book. The Hopis had a prophet many, many years ago when they came up from the Underworld, and he knew all about the white men. Of the four chiefs who came up from under the ground, the eldest had no faults. He was sent to the east and told to bow down to the sun, and, when he returned, it was prophesied that his children would overspread the earth. That man was the white man and that is why the Hopis have always been our friends. The first chief prophesied that when the Faultless One returned, a new world would begin at Kahwestimah."

She paused, her eyes radiant, and, as a silence fell upon them, the Hopi took up the tale.

"Never has been told before," he stated. "But it is all painted on a rock. On the cliff at Red Mesa the great chief made a picture, which only my people know. It shows in a prophecy the white man, riding a horse, and the Hopi bowing down, making this sign across his neck." He drew his hand across his throat significantly and looked up at Lord Benedict with a smile. "Would you like to see that rock? I will take you right to the place."

"Well, I . . . ah . . . fear," began the colonel after a glance at Major Doyle, "that under the circumstances it will be impossible. We shall be going on in the morning, when the wagon train departs."

"But . . . why, Father?" cried Lady Grace. "I thought it was all settled that we should see this wonderful Snake Dance. Harold's father is the snake chief and he will gain us permission to photograph the dance."

"Never has been done before," observed Harold, and the major turned on him roughly.

"Who invited you here," he demanded, "to come and sit on my porch? Didn't I tell you to get out of town?"

"Lady asked me," replied the Hopi, smiling easily, and Grace took up the cudgels.

"Why, yes, Major," she said, "I came out for air, while you and *Pater* talked, and Harold has been entertaining me. He's really a wonderful boy, and I hope you won't mind. He had no intention to intrude."

Harold folded his smooth brown arms and gazed away pensively, and the major scratched his head.

"Well, he had his orders . . . ," he began, then scowled, and clumped into the house.

"He has such a nice name," went on Lady Grace admiringly. "Polinuivah . . . Chasing Butterflies. Harold Chasing Butterflies . . . isn't that sweet and poetic? And he has learned to speak English perfectly."

"Ah . . . yes, but even so, I am afraid, my dear, we

will not be able to make the trip. Major Doyle assures me that, even on the emigrant trail, the road is not wholly without danger. And, much as I should love to witness this Snake Dance, he advises me not to go."

"I will take you myself," promised Harold glibly, "and then you will be perfectly safe. My father is chief at Red Mesa. Everyone has to do what he says. My people are called Peace People. They do not fight and kill, like the Apaches and bad Paiutes and Navajos. They love all people who are friends."

"Nevertheless," returned Lord Benedict, "we shall be compelled to go on. It has been reported to Major Doyle that certain of the Peace People have raided the wagons of the white people, and, until that is cleared up, he will permit no traffic into your country."

"That is bad Paiutes," complained Harold. "They live on Highest Mountain . . . many cañons . . . and no one can go in, only them. They get our bows and arrows. They come through my country. Then they kill some poor people and carry off some women and soldiers blame it on us."

"I must see the major again," decided Colonel Benedict as his daughter raised her eyebrows. "Surely with all these troops, and the Navajo scouts as well, he could spare us a sufficient escort."

"Not the Navajos," advised Harold hastily. "All they know is to steal something. They are enemies of the Peace People. When my people raised corn, the Navajos came and took it. They drove off our sheep and goats. Then, six years ago, the soldiers came and caught them . . . all those bad, fighting Navajos that steal our corn! They took them far away and kept them four years, and then they let them come back. That is why they hate my people.

We are friends of the white men . . . always. Everything that was bound to happen we knew, long ago. We knew the soldiers would come. But our great chief made a prophecy not to fight them and something good would happen. So when the bad Navajos came and killed my people, Washington was very angry. He sent in his soldiers and they chased them all away. Now the Navajos are mad at us."

"I will consult Major Doyle," said his lordship, and went back into the house.

"You will be safe." Harold nodded, smiling up at Lady Grace. "All ladies in my country are safe. Only Navajos and Apaches and bad Paiutes steal them. You come . . . I will show you something beautiful. Wonderful story, acted out every year. How lady came from north and man from south and met on Red Mesa, my home. This lady have heavy burden on back. But man . . . he young man . . . strong! He take basket off . . . lady look up . . . she smile. She like him. Bimeby they married."

"Oh, wonderful," she sighed. "An ancient play."

"You come," he coaxed, and, as the men stepped out, he was patting her on the arm.

"What the devil are you doing?" demanded the major indignantly. Then he glanced at Lord Benedict and stood up very straight. "I am very sorry," he said, turning to Lady Grace, "but I cannot give my consent."

"Not if we have an escort?" she protested. "Surely the danger is very little among these Peace People . . . and Harold will be responsible for our safety."

"That's just it," answered the major. "What about Harold? I have had him in the guardhouse twice already, for disobeying my orders."

"Very sorry," observed Harold, smiling.

"Oh, and they have an ancient play. He was telling me all about it. How the north people and the south people joined. It is like an old miracle play . . . an allegory."

"Confound the beggar," grumbled her father. "Well, I leave it to you, Major Doyle."

"Bring me Silver Hat!" rapped out the major to his orderly, and turned to pace the porch.

The scout rose from the group of Navajos who sat resting under the cottonwoods that lined the blood-red river, and, as he strode toward them, Harold Polinuivah shrank away.

"Silver Hat," began Doyle, "this lady and gentleman have been placed in my care by Washington and they want to go into Kahwestimah. You've just come back from that country . . . do you think it is perfectly safe?"

The keen blue eyes shifted from Major Doyle to Colonel Benedict, from Lady Grace to the diminished Hopi. "No, sir," he said at last.

"Not even with an escort?" asked his lordship.

"No, sir," returned the scout.

"Well, why not?" challenged Lady Grace. "It certainly seems strange to me that a detail of soldiers cannot take us to the Snake Dance in safety. Aren't the Hopis a peaceful people?"

He glanced at Harold and smiled. "Yes," he said. "But they raid wagon trains, too."

"How do you know?" she came back sharply.

"That's my business . . . guarding the trail," he answered. "We found their tracks, going back."

"My people do not kill!" defended Harold, rising up with a venomous hiss. "That was done by bad

Paiutes who ride through our country, to lay all their
raids on us. The Hopis love all who are friends."

Silver Hat looked him over and shrugged his
shoulders.

"We are Peace People!" quavered Polinuivah.

"Well, what about it, Silver Hat?" inquired Doyle
expectantly, and Lady Grace eyed him hopefully.
She had not forgotten his affront of the early morning, when he had refused to stand beside her and be
photographed, and she could see by the way he
turned away from Harold that there was no love between them. Yet she had set her mind on this trip to
far Kahwestimah, where in masks and ancient
pageantry the north woman and the south man met
to symbolize the beginning of a race. Every word
that Harold had said added its mite to the spell that
the very name Kahwestimah cast over her, but this
one man stood in her way.

Big and dominant in his broad sombrero, on
which in chased silver the Mexican eagle grasped a
snake in its claws, she could see how her father, and
even Major Doyle, had passed the onus to him, and
she knew he would not fail them. Like the red-
flowing Rio Bravo that barred the way to the north,
he was an elemental force, oblivious to her charms.
She had even sensed a fierce resistance to her will in
the scornful way he had said no. Now, as they
waited to hear his answer to Polinuivah, she read a
somber hatred in his eyes.

"Ask him," he said, "what the Peace People did to
the Navajo women and children at Five Buttes."

"That is lie!" cried Harold, suddenly beside himself with rage. "The Navajos are cuthroats . . . they

rob the Hopis of everything. It was prophesied that my people should repay them."

"Is that why the Hopis killed them?" asked Silver Hat.

Harold forgot his poise. "Yes!" he snapped, backing up.

"Then you are not Peace People," answered Silver Hat. "You are murderers. You kill women and children."

"The spirits came to Loloma," clamored Harold in a frenzy, "and told him the time would come. Then the soldiers and Kit Carson drove the Navajos among us and we knew it was the will of the gods. We helped the Great Chief at Washington to conquer our ancient enemies. But that is all over now. The Navajos stay away. All is peace in Kahwestimah. The country is perfectly safe."

"Then where are the three white women that the Hopis captured on the bank of the Dry Cimarrón? I saw the tracks myself, and they led to Red Mesa. There were Hopi arrows in the dead."

Harold Chasing Butterflies reared back, his clenched jaws bulging out like the head of a rattlesnake as he pointed a trembling finger at his enemy. "You are nothing but a Navajo yourself," he said. "That is why you tell lies about my people."

"You call me a liar?" flared back Silver Hat, and with a swift, contemptuous blow he slapped him down and wiped his hand on his knee.

"That will do," spoke up Doyle, stepping in. "I knew the truth would come out. There will be no trips across the Rio Bravo until this woman-stealing business is cleared up. You, Harold Polinuivah, go back to your father and tell him that Washington is watching him. Tell him the Big Chief has given me orders to tear down his village if another woman is touched. Now get out of town and don't you come back or I'll throw you into the guardhouse."

Harold Chasing Butterflies rose up from where he lay and stared about with gleaming eyes. Then he turned toward Kahwestimah, breaking into a tireless trot as he fell into the deeply worn trail. At the ford of the Rio Bravo he stopped and took off his moccasins before he splashed across the turbulent stream, and Lady Grace watched him wistfully.

Above the swell of the red sand hills Highest Mountain raised its pinnacles, the far mesas cast deep, mysterious shadows, and on the last summit he turned and looked back, throwing up a thin arm imperiously. The major grunted, Silver Hat and Colonel Benedict stood mutely, but in a quick, ecstatic sweep Lady Grace waved back and fled to the silence of her room.

CHAPTER THREE

Silver Hat and Jani, his Navajo brother, rode the ridge far above the emigrant trail.

"She cried," said Jani, "so they say."

Silver Hat stopped his horse and gazed long at a wagon train, rolling slowly into the west.

"Nevertheless," he answered, "she is there, with her father. That is better than what we have seen."

"The frowzy-headed Hopi wanted to steal her," observed Jani. "What a pleasure to cut his heart out! But, now, Washington Natani has ordered us to spare them, and the Monkey People will laugh when we pass. It is too late to kill them, I think."

"I have a knife here," said Silver Hat, "for Polinuivah, the Butterfly Chaser, if he lays hands on another white woman."

"Did you see him bow and smile and pat the arm of Slender Woman? Iron Tooth Natani was very angry. But none of the white men could drive him away until you slapped his face."

"It was the woman!" accused Silver Hat. "She

caused it all. She was just as my grandfather, the
venerable deceased Long Beard, always told me the
white women are. When they smile and are very
beautiful and make all men do their will, he told me
never to look at them. It was one like that who drove
him from his people and made him hide till he died
in these mountains. And on his way across the
plains, he found me, running away, and took me for
his son."

"He was a good man," said Jani, "and bought me
from the Hopis when they kept me for a slave. But,
now he is gone, I am your slave."

"You are my brother," responded Silver Hat.
"And I, too, hate the Hopis for killing your mother
at Five Buttes. When I threw that in his teeth, the lying Butterfly Chaser said no more about the Louse
Heads being Peace People."

"They are witches!" cried Jani. "That is why they
love peace. They kill their enemies by witchcraft."

"Chief Iron Tooth is afraid for Slender Woman
yet," observed Silver Hat, drawing out his spyglass.
"He told me to guard her past the country of the
Hopis and clear into the land of the Walapais. It is
for some devil worship that they steal these golden
women. But now Slender Woman hates me, for slap-
ping Polinuivah, so I must watch her wagon from
here."

He focused his spyglass on the trim yellow wagon
that followed in the wake of the ox teams. It was
built like an ambulance, but with the body enclosed
and lockers along the sides, and within it Lord
Benedict had a rack for his guns and everything put
in its place.

"I can see her," announced Silver Hat. "She is

walking by the wagon. The dust from the big teams has driven them far back. But Iron Tooth told them not to stop."

"If the Hopis see her walking, they will want to steal her," suggested Jani. "Then what will my brother do?"

"We will ride on to our cabin," said Silver Hat, "where I can look through the big telescope that my grandfather used, to watch the trails for his enemies."

"He must have killed many men," murmured Jani admiringly, "to have them follow him so far."

"Only one," replied Silver Hat. "But he was a great chief. That is why they tried to find him. But no one ever knew of this cabin where we go, nor of the other across the river in Kahwestimah. My grandfather remained in hiding while I went to the fort and traded our furs for supplies. But not until yesterday did I fully believe what he told me of the ways of women. Not all women, my brother, but those who are beautiful, like this Slender Woman from across the Eastern Ocean. It was from women like her that he told me to flee . . . never to look at them . . . always to say no. And now Chief Iron Tooth has ordered me to guard her, but never to let her know. I must ride far away, always watching her wagon, seeing her close as I look through my glass. But never, unless the Hopis seek to steal her, will I speak to Estsan Tsosi again."

"Are you sad?" asked Jani at last.

"*Hola!*" answered Silver Hat. "I do not know!" And he put his horse to a lope. Up and down rough trails that only deer and elk used he spurred on till he came to a cliff, and there among the trees in a little sunlit space stood the cabin where Selah Grainger had lived. Jani tended the horses and started a fire while eagerly, like a man in a fever, Silver Hat set up his telescope. Then he swept the valley below until, crawling slowly among the junipers, he found the emigrant train. But the yellow spring wagon with its fast-stepping mules no longer dragged along in the dust.

Silver Hat swung his glass on its swivel and looked out the road, far ahead. Then he followed the trail backward until in a little cañon he caught a yellow glint. They had stopped by the narrow stream to soak their dried-out wheels—but Major Doyle had forbidden them to stop! Silver Hat watched intently as Colonel Benedict, bucket by bucket, poured water over his wheels, while a golden head in the shade of a juniper marked the spot where Slender Woman slept.

"Saddle our horses!" he shouted to Jani, and with a long, slow sweep of the telescope he followed the cañon down to its junction with the river. The Rio Bravo spread out in silvery arabesques among the sandbars it had lain down in flood, and each blast of the west wind snatched up dust from its dry bed and whirled it up into the sky. But across the river in Kahwestimah a point of dust moved toward them— against the wind, with bobbing heads in the lead.

"There come the Hopis!" he announced, and ran out to leap on his horse. Jani whirled in behind, and they dashed down the long ridge, but as they sighted the wagon, they stopped. Everything was as before; only some half-naked Indian boys were gathered about the camp.

"They are begging," said Silver Hat, passing the

glass to Jani. "But tell me, are they Paiutes or Hopis?"

"Hopis," answered Jani, "and Slender Woman is giving them something."

"That is bad," responded Silver Hat. "They will never go now. Even the children of the Monkey People are treacherous."

He sat down on a rock that overlooked the cañon and watched Slender Woman through his spyglass. She stood among them distributing gifts like Ceres, the goddess of plenty, but, although she put candy and fruit into every outstretched hand, they followed at her heels insistently. Scrawny arms were raised higher; their black heads shook menacingly. Then with a rush they set upon her, dragging her down with one quick jerk, and Silver Hat ran for his horse. It had come so naturally that he could hardly believe his eyes, until suddenly he saw her golden head go down. Spiteful hands had laid hold of her glorious hair, impish figures had swarmed over her like ants, and in a flash every child was running and striking as if transformed into a demon.

"The little devils!" cursed Silver Hat, spurring his racehorse at every bound, but, although he rode like the wind, he arrived too late to save her from their desecrating hands. They were fighting over her body like hounds above a kill. Every rag of her clothing was gone. While some dragged her by the hair across the rough and thorny ground, others snatched at her feet. The most malevolent of all was clutching her by the throat as Silver Hat dashed among them, and he kicked him with all his strength. Then his quirt came down on each dodging, squirming back, and they scattered among the brush like quail.

Beneath the wagon, his head bloodied by rocks, Lord Benedict lay like one dead, while within it, unaware of the panic outside, Hopis quarreled over the spoils like magpies. Among these whirled Jani when, left behind in the race, he came spurring upon the scene of the attack. With his pistol for a club he belted them right and left, chasing after them as they fled from his wrath. Then suddenly all were gone and Silver Hat dropped down to lift Lady Grace from the ground.

She had fainted and all the aura of her beauty had left her. Her hair was tangled, her face bruised, her body a mass of thorns where the needle grass had entered her flesh. When he bore her to the brook and dashed water on her, she came back to life with a moan.

"What is it?" she cried as she roused up and looked about. "Where am I? What has happened?"

"You are hurt," he said, washing the grime from her face and plucking out a thorn.

At that her memory came back. "Oh, look at me," she sobbed, "without a rag of clothes on! Did they do all this? Those boys? Oh, the ignominy of it! To fight over me like animals! And after I had given them presents!"

"They were Hopis," replied Silver Hat. "The Peace People. But I was watching them from the ridge."

He rose up and went back to where Jani was, and she clutched at a blanket on the ground. Her possessions were scattered everywhere, just as the Hopis had dropped them, and she drew the blanket across her breast. But at its touch a thousand thorns stung her flesh and she shuddered and lifted it off.

"The Hopi men are coming," said Silver Hat, rushing up. Before she could cry out, he wrapped the blanket about her and started for his horse. There was a quick ecstasy of pain as he raised her to the saddle and leaped swiftly up behind. Then he took her in his arms and vaulted into her place, and his mount sprang away at a gallop. Behind them, as they fled, they could hear the *whang* of a rifle as Jani held back the foe, but soon there was nothing but the agony of her wounds to remind Lady Grace of her shame. She had been beaten by beggars, stripped of everything in an instant, and now she was being carried away.

Up the mountain ridge they plunged, dodging and turning among the trees, but as the tired horse slowed down and she became conscious of her plight, she struggled to escape. Every inch of her body seemed full of broken thorns that the blanket forced in farther, but, although she shuddered in his grasp, her captor held her fast, still spurring on up the ridge. Then, at last, he lay her down on a bed and she stared about, bewildered. He stood above her, dark and grim, looking her over with cold blue eyes, and she burst into helpless tears.

CHAPTER FOUR

By the platform built in front of the cabin window, Silver Hat stood peering through his telescope. Although his eye swept the valley and came to rest on the looted wagon, he was only conscious of a woman crying. His adoptive father, Grainger, had told him of this weakness, but never before had he heard it. He looked again through the clean-focused glass, and on the emigrant trail he saw a cavalry patrol.

"The soldiers are coming!" he said, and she started up in alarm.

"What? Here?" she cried. "Oh, do not let them see me! Only hide me until they are gone!"

"No, no. Down on the road," he replied. "I can see your father, standing up."

"Poor *Pater*," she sighed. "Did they beat him and strip him, too? Oh, the miserable creatures . . . after all we had done for them. Just look at the thorns in my hands."

She held them out and he glanced back reluctantly, before turning again to the telescope.

"Here comes Jani," he announced. "Up the ridge."

"Please send him away," she begged. "Oh, the shame of it. The shame! How can I ever pluck out these thorns and forget the indignity of it all?"

"Never mind," he said. "I'll take care of you. Shall I send Jani down to report?"

"No, no," she wept miserably. "They must know nothing. Nothing! Only keep me hid until my wounds are healed and I can make me some woman's clothes."

"But your father will be anxious. The soldiers will hunt everywhere. Major Doyle will expect me to report."

"If they come, I shall die," she wailed in despair. "Oh, these thorns!" She shuddered with pain.

"Just lie down," he soothed, "and I'll rub you with bear oil. Then, after the thorns have softened, I'll pull them out of your back."

She stretched out obediently and, slowly and gently, he rubbed her quivering flesh with the oil. The rough rocks had bruised her, there were marks of impish scratches, and from head to foot her satiny skin was thrust full of the poisonous needle grass.

"Take a big drink of this," he said at last, fetching out a bottle of brandy. Then with quick, effective twitches he plucked out the thorns while she lay with her face turned away. Only the tense set of her jaw, the involuntary flinching, revealed that she was not in a faint. After a few minutes of work he put aside his knife and stepped out, closing the door behind him.

Jani stood by the cabin, his eyes big with wonder, but Silver Hat evaded his gaze. "She is full of thorns," he said. "I am helping to pull them out. But no one must know she is here."

"Yes, *shihchai*," responded Jani respectfully.

"We will camp by the cliff," went on Silver Hat. "The Hopis tore off all her clothes. But what did you find when the warriors came up? Was Harold Polinuivah among them?"

"I could not see him. They ran away when I shot my rifle at them."

"And her father. Was he hurt?"

"Only his head, where they struck him with rocks."

"The soldiers have come," went on Silver Hat. "They will take him to the fort. But now it is the wish of Slender Woman that no one shall know she is here."

He turned and went inside, and there on the bed Slender Woman sat plucking out the thorns, while miserable tears ran down her cheeks.

"Oh, the shame of it," she moaned as she turned her face away. "How can I bear to wear clothes?"

"I will stretch a curtain," he answered, "and leave you to yourself. Use plenty of bear oil and take a drink when it hurts. Jani and I will camp outside."

He hung blankets across the room and stepped outside again, and Jani looked up at him curiously.

"Light a fire," directed Silver Hat, "where the smoke will not show. She will be here many days."

"But what of Chief Iron Tooth? He will think she is dead unless I signal with smoke."

"She is ashamed," explained Silver Hat, "because

she was stripped by the vile Hopi boys. So she will hide here until she is well."

"But Iron Tooth will be angry. He will search all the mesas to see where the Hopis have hid her."

"Nevertheless," stated Silver Hat, "that is her wish. Perhaps, if Iron Tooth is angry, he will tear down Polinuivah's village."

"Good!" Jani grinned. "Silver Hat says well. But was it not the advice of your venerable, deceased grandfather always to answer the white women with no?"

She is like a child now," responded Silver Hat at last. "She weeps and plucks out the thorns. When she is well and strong again, and we have made her some woman's clothes, I will remember what my grandfather has said."

"*Yáhehteh . . .* good!" Jani nodded, but the wondering look had come back into his eyes.

He watched and listened day by day as his brother came and went—cooking food and carrying it in, soaking sinews to sew buckskin, but never did he hear Silver Hat say no. At the fort, when she was beautiful and all the white men deferred to her, Silver Hat had stood up against Slender Woman. She had wanted his picture, standing beside her arm in arm, but he had let Harold Polinuivah pose. When she had overridden them all in her desire to cross the river into Kahwestimah, it was Silver Hat who had told her no. But now he said nothing, going in and out in silence, and Jani held his tongue.

From the buttes in the great desert on the other side of the Río Bravo he saw smoke signals mount to the sky. The Navajo scouts were out with the sol-

diers, making smoke talks back to the fort. They
were searching the Hopi country for some trace of
Slender Woman, but all the time she was hidden in
their cabin. Iron Tooth Natani would fly into a rage
when he learned how his own scouts had deceived
him, but Silver Hat did nothing when he read by
their tall smokes how his brothers, the Navajos, suffered. The woman had broken his will. She had
made him like the rest. The venerable, deceased
Long Beard had spoken well, but his grandson had
forgotten.

Nine days passed and still the signal smokes rose
and patrols galloped off down the emigrant trail,
but in her cabin boudoir Lady Grace nursed her
wounds and sewed her Indian clothes. First, to
cover her shame, she had draped her body in soft
doeskins, tying the feet over her shoulders for fas-
tenings, but, as the agony of her hurts abated, she
cut out a skirt and tunic. Then Jani was summoned
in to fit her for Navajo moccasins and now she was
fully clothed.

To each moccasin foot was attached four arm
lengths of soft buckskin, which she wrapped
around and around, making trim white leggings,
fastened with red yarn garters at the knees. A fine
fringe decorated the hem of her *conchas*, but still,
while Silver Hat fretted and watched the trail, she
postponed the hour of her return.

"I must forget," she said. "It is like a bad dream."

And so the days passed. Like Penelope, unravel-
ing at night what she had woven the day before in
order to put off her suitors, she seemed to Silver Hat
to seek more tasks to do rather than ride back and
face the world. Each morning, blushing deeply and

turning her face away, she had him pluck the thorns from her back. They had stuck in deeply, leaving tiny barbed points that worked out through the tender skin, and with a grim face that never changed he picked them out with his sheath knife until the last angry spot had healed—healed and lost its redness, leaving her back a vision of beauty—but still she put off the day.

"Do I look well?" she demanded anxiously as he entered the cabin one morning to search the valley through his telescope. As she asked him, Lady Grace smiled. Her spirits had returned, and the once-scarred face was radiant with a new, appealing glow, but something in her eyes bade Silver Hat beware, and he drew down his brows, saying nothing.

"It is your fault," she chided, "if I ask you every morning. For you know I have no mirror."

"You look fine," he responded, passing on. "But what's all this . . . down below?"

He focused the long glass and drew a line on the emigrant trail, and Lady Grace came close beside him.

"Let me look," she said gaily, "at these gallant soldiers who seek a lost maiden in distress."

"They have come back to the spot . . . with scouts," he said. "They are cutting circles to find our tracks."

She peered through the telescope and sighed.

"So we must go," she said at last.

"And why not?" he demanded impatiently. "Think of your father at the fort! Think of the major and all the scouts! But I know what has sent them back. They have torn down every house in old Masawa's pueblo and they know that you're not there."

"What? In Polinuivah's village?" she gasped. "Why didn't you tell me before?"

"Would you have gone in," he asked, "if I had?"

"I couldn't." She shuddered. "You don't know how I felt about it. What? With my face all scratched and bruised? Without a stitch of clothing, and my body like a pincushion filled with thorns? But I'm sorry for poor Harold."

"You don't need to be," he answered. "He was behind all this devilment. And unless he hid on the top of Highest Mountain, I'll bet he's in the guardhouse right now."

"In the guardhouse? Why, what for?"

"Didn't you hear what Major Doyle said to him when he ordered him to go back home? He said, if another white woman was molested on the trail, he'd come out and tear down their village and put poor Harold in the guardhouse."

"Why, Silver Hat," she cried reproachfully, "this is downright spiteful! Those naked little beggars were not Hopis at all. They told me themselves they were Paiutes."

"Well, Jani was raised in Kahwestimah and he says they were Hopis. But we'll soon find out when we see the scouts. They back-tracked them the next day. I know."

"You mean . . . traced them back to their homes?"

"That's our orders, when a woman is attacked. The government is tired of fooling with these Hopis. And with you missing, the major would act."

Lady Grace looked again through the telescope at the patient scouts cutting for sign.

"We must go," she decided. "I am sorry for this. But everything can be explained."

"I'll bring up the horses," responded Silver Hat with alacrity, but she stopped him as he reached the door.

"Let Jani go," she said softly. "I want to speak with you . . . Silver Hat."

He turned and looked at her, his eyes narrowing suspiciously, and she reached out and took his hand.

"Please," she coaxed, and after a moment's indecision he spoke to Jani and closed the door.

"No, not there," she insisted as he started for the window. "Are you angry with me, Silver Hat? After being such a loyal friend? Then sit down with me here."

He glanced at her strangely and sat down on the bed where for days they had gone through their strange rites—he plucking with his sheath knife at the stubborn thorns, she enduring without a moan. They had worked together grimly, neither speaking their hidden thoughts, but now she was holding his hand.

"It is strange," she said, "how we have been thrown together. But now it will soon be all over. When we return to the fort, I shall be Lady Grace and you simply Silver Hat, the scout. But before we go, I must thank you for saving me from those creatures. You have been very gentle and kind, and now you must help me to forget. Never speak to me again of those despicable beggars who subjected me to that indignity. Never reveal to a soul what happened to me. And order Jani to hold his tongue. When I go back to the fort, I shall inform my father that I was suffering from a severe nervous shock. I was rescued by you and lay hidden in this cabin until my strength and poise were restored. I want no one in the world to know what has happened . . . it must

remain between us three. Is that asking too much . . .
for a friend?"

She looked up at him earnestly, her eyes dark with
a strange glow, and suddenly his reserve fell away.

"No, indeed," he said. "I will never tell anyone.
And Jani will keep his mouth shut. The Navajos are
great gossips, but he and I are brothers. I know his
secret name. Anything that I ask of him, when I
speak that holy name, he must do for me even if he
dies."

"How strange," she murmured. "The knights of
the Round Table had such an oath between them,
and here it is found among savages. Have you told
your secret name to him?"

"No. Jani is my brother, but he was the slave of my
adopted father, and, when I freed him, he gave me
his name. That is the custom among warriors who
have been beaten in battle. They reveal their secret
name and become slaves, to keep from being
killed."

"But are you free?" she asked, smiling archly.

"I am a free scout!" he answered. "I take orders
from no one. Even Iron Tooth asks me to go."

"And was it at his request that you followed our
wagon? Or was it by your own will?"

"It was at his request," he responded gravely.

"But you did not object?" she persisted. "It was
not against your will?"

"No," he said. "I knew you were in danger. That is
my business . . . I guard the trail."

"And you did not love me, nor follow for my sake?
There was nothing like that behind it? Then, now, I
begin to understand." She laughed softly to herself,
taking his hand caressingly, holding it lightly, laying

it down. "What a man," she murmured. "And have I come so far to find my Galahad?"

"What do you mean?" he asked at last.

"Dear boy," she said, "when you were working on my back, I called you my iron man. Never even by a look or a touch of the hand did you remind me that I was a woman. I am going far away and will never come back. You will never see me again. Will you give me a kiss . . . to remember you by? Or are you made of stone?"

She leaned against him, smiling, gazing deeply into his blue eyes, drawing his stern, rebellious head down and down, until suddenly he caught her up and kissed her again and again while she struggled and fought to go free. Then she pulled away and with a resounding slap struck him angrily across the face.

"Keep your place!" she commanded haughtily. "Do you think I want that from you?"

He drew back, his cheek burning, and regarded her intently like a bronco buster eying an untamed filly, but she did not quail before him. Generations of noble blood rose up to steel her heart, and so their stern anger flashed back and forth like heat lightning between earth and sky.

"By rights," he said at last, "I ought to slap you back, but that is not our way out here. And, besides, I ought to be glad. My grandfather told me that all women were like you, but somehow I could not believe it. He came here to get away from a woman . . . a beautiful woman, who had ruined his life. She led him on . . . the way you did . . . and then she slapped his face. But you will never slap my face again."

Lady Grace drew back, abashed by his rebuke,

and, as she faced him, her swift anger died. "I am sorry," she said, "and I hope, my friend, you will not think me wholly ungrateful. I shall never forget your kindness . . . and, when we return to the fort, my father will reward you bountifully."

"To hell with him!" he answered roughly. "This slap in the face is the reward I'll remember."

He stepped out the door at the sound of horses running and Lady Grace stood alone in the cabin. She gazed about at each familiar thing—the buckskins, the gay blankets, the bed. Then tears came to her eyes and she bowed her head, weeping. But when she came out, she was calm.

CHAPTER FIVE

The return to the fort was in silence. Lady Grace had often read of the North American Indians and how they treaded the primeval forests without making a sound for hours. The free scout, Silver Hat, led the way through the trees, avoiding all trails where their horse tracks would show, circling far to lead the soldiers from the cabin. And then, around a bend, they came upon Fort Defiance, and a welcome that almost frightened her. There was a shout, a running of men, and like one saved from the dead she was borne into the presence of her father. Lord Benedict had waited long for some bearer of good news to inform him that his daughter was found, but when she appeared before him, garbed in buckskin like an Indian and the picture of radiant health, he was overcome with astonishment.

"Why, dearest," he exclaimed, "where have you been all the while? Were you carried away by the Hopis?"

"Why, no, *Pater*," she replied, "I have been in

good hands. I am very sorry, indeed, to have kept you in suspense, but I have been resting, to recover from the shock."

"Aren't you injured in any way? We found signs of a terrific struggle."

"Not in the least," she answered. "Only my clothes were badly torn. So, while I was recovering, Silver Hat and Jani supplied the buckskin and I made this . . . with my own hands."

She displayed her trim suit proudly and ran to embrace her father, but even his joy at her homecoming was tempered by a baffled surprise. "Well, upon my word," he gasped. "I can hardly believe my eyes. Here we have scouted the country without finding a sign of you for well upon eleven days. And the scene at the wagon was such that we might well have imagined the worst. Will you kindly explain how you chanced to escape and . . . ah, here she is, Major Doyle."

He turned with a broad smile to the astounded major, and Lady Grace greeted him prettily, but after his first relief at finding her alive Doyle's rugged features turned grim.

"What's this?" he barked, casting a glance at the Navajo moccasins, the trim skirt, and silver-trimmed tunic. "Have the Navajos been keeping you hid? My scouts have been hunting you everywhere."

"It was two of your scouts who rescued me," she responded with a placating smile. "But on account of my clothes being torn . . ."

"Then why didn't they report?" he rapped out.

"Because," she answered evenly, "I forbade them to do so until I had recovered from the shock."

"You could have recovered at the fort!" he exploded. "My soldiers and scouts have ridden down their horses, and now you come back like this."

He looked her up and down, from her neat moccasins to her wind-blown hair, and Lady Grace drew herself up proudly.

"In what condition, may I ask," she demanded, "would you prefer to have me return?"

"Yes, yes," broke in her father, "we should be very thankful that my daughter has escaped so fortunately. And if you have suffered any loss of animals, I shall be only too glad to replace them."

"Damn the animals!" burst out the major. "It's my nerves that I'm talking about. You were placed in my care by the State Department at Washington, and by your own willful negligence you were attacked by these Indians after I had warned you to stay close to the train. Then . . ."

"That is a subject we can discuss at some other time," replied his lordship with a haughty bow. "My dear child," he went on kindly, "you can hardly imagine how happy we are to see you back, safe and sound. I was struck on the head by those impudent young savages and quite knocked out for the moment, and, when I recovered consciousness, you had entirely disappeared. Then the soldiers came and found the signs of the struggle and . . . well, really, we believed you were lost. But would you mind telling us . . . and especially Major Doyle . . . in what way you made your escape?"

Lady Grace bowed her head, while the crowd stood silently in order to catch every word.

"I cannot tell you," she said, "more than this . . . that I, too, was struck on the head. When I recovered consciousness, I was in a mountain cabin and Silver

Hat, the scout, was bending over me. He informed me later that, by the major's orders, he had been watching our wagon from the heights and at the first sign of an attack he had charged down and rescued me. That is all I can tell."

"Well, bravo, Major!" cried Lord Benedict. "Your scouts have shown their mettle, after all. I must see this young man and reward him handsomely. That was very good work, indeed."

"Bring me Silver Hat," ordered Major Doyle, looking straight ahead, "and we'll get to the bottom of this. No scout of mine can keep me waiting ten days to humor the whim of some woman. His orders were to report, and on account of his negligence . . ."

"No, Major," broke in Lady Grace, "I must assume the responsibility for all that. I had received a great shock and was hardly myself. My mind seemed to totter on its throne. So, to preserve my own sanity, I begged him as a gentleman to allow me to rest and forget."

"A very wise thing to do, under the circumstances." Her father nodded. "I heartily approve of his actions."

"Bring him in!" thundered Major Doyle as his orderly delayed, and at last the soldier returned.

"Sorry, sir," he said, saluting, "but Silver Hat is gone."

"Gone where?" demanded the major.

"He and his Indian rode away as soon as they came in. They took the trail to the south."

"Captain Northcutt," snapped Major Doyle, "put some scouts on his trail. It is his duty to return and report. Order Desteen to make signal smokes and recall all our men. Now, Miss Benedict, one question more. Who were these Indians that attacked your wagon? They were Hopi boys, of course."

"No, Major," she answered firmly, "they were Paiutes. They told me so themselves."

"They were Hopis!" declared Major Doyle. "That was Polinuivah's work and I've got him in the guardhouse right now."

"Certainly not!" she cried. "They were beggarly little creatures, and not like Polinuivah at all. But I brought it on myself. I offered them candy, until at last they became insistent and finally attacked me from behind. But they were vile, filthy imps ... mere savages. I wish Harold released at once."

"I'll consider that, later," returned the major. "After I've talked with Silver Hat and Jani. Will you kindly describe these Indians?"

"Major Doyle," began Lady Grace, "this whole affair has been humiliating to me in the extreme. It is something I wish to forget. So I must ask you not to question me further."

"Yes, yes," spoke up her father, "she has suffered a great shock. Come along to your room, my darling ... it shall never be referred to again. And Major, when Silver Hat returns, I must see him and reward him for his kindness."

He led his daughter away and Major Doyle rushed out to hasten the search for his scout, but in the morning, when Lady Grace stepped out on the verandah, Silver Hat had not returned. On the cliff behind the fort a thin line of smoke rose straight up, and, as she watched it, a tall Indian threw a green cedar top on the flames and cast his blanket upon it. Then as the white smoke was confined, he released it suddenly in a single, balloon-like puff. It was

Desteen, the old Navajo medicine man, and, as he made smoke talk, Major Doyle came out.

"He's signaling to Silver Hat," he grumbled, and fell to pacing the porch. "Miss Benedict," he said at last, "now that you've had a night's sleep and recovered your usual health, I believe you owe it to me to answer a few simple questions. I am not acquainted with the ways of the nobility, and perhaps in England this would be considered quite all right, but it seemed to me yesterday from the way you shut me up that you were endeavoring to conceal certain things. Well, that is all right as far as you personally are concerned. You have made me a lot of trouble, but you'll soon be off my hands, and, if you wish to forget, you may. But don't you think it is taxing hospitality rather far to drive my best scout away?"

"You mean Silver Hat?" she asked.

"Yes, I do. And now answer me this: Did you have a quarrel with him?"

A blush mounted her rosy cheeks as she turned her face away. "Well . . . yes," she said at last.

"I knew it," he growled, and fell to pacing the floor again. "My best man," he muttered, "worth a hundred regular scouts. Speaks four languages . . . knows all the trails. Don't you think you ought to help me get him back? And don't forget . . . he saved your life."

"No, I know," she faltered. "Oh, Major, I can't forget. But how can we bring him back? I was so inconsiderate . . . I didn't even thank him. And he was always so obliging and kind."

"In love with you, of course," grumbled the major cynically, but Lady Grace shook her head.

"Not in the slightest," she stated. "A perfect gentleman in every way, but he always kept his place."

"Uhhr," grunted Doyle, "so that was where you differed . . . you expected him to keep his place. Well, let me tell you, Miss Benedict, out here in Arizona we have no places to keep. Every man is his own master, and the Queen of England couldn't make him act the flunky. In all the years that Silver Hat has been working for me, I have never given him a direct order."

"Really?" she cried. "I noticed from the first that he rather neglected to salute."

"Man to man." The major nodded. "That's the only way to handle them. These free scouts are a class by themselves. They're worth a hundred soldiers when it comes to a crisis, but they wouldn't touch their hat to a king."

"I'm sorry," she said contritely, "if I have ever unintentionally made some reference to rank or class. In this country, of course, you are all free and equal. But he was always so deferential . . . so polite."

"He's a gentleman," declared Major Doyle. "Comes from a good family . . . back East. And raised by a gentleman, out here. I never met Selah Grainger but once, but you could see he was a thoroughbred."

"Did he . . . have some trouble?" she suggested, and suddenly the major turned grim.

"Not that I know of," he denied. "And while he lived in these hills, he saved the lives of hundreds of emigrants. The government learned to know that when Grainger sent a warning, the Indians were about to strike. But now that he is dead, we depend on Silver Hat. What was it that you quarreled about?"

He shot the question at her sharply and for once Lady Grace forgot her pride.

"I don't know," she answered miserably. "It was just before we left and I . . . I slapped him in the face."

"My God!" exclaimed Major Doyle. "No wonder he disappeared. Well, if you really want to help . . . he'll never come back as long as you're at the fort."

"Do you . . . want me to go?" she faltered. "I'd like to thank him, and bid him good-bye. And he gave me this beautiful buckskin, too. Don't you think he would come, if I waited?"

"Never in the world," declared the major. "And, Miss Benedict, I need that man."

"Yes, I know." She nodded, and stood gazing far away at a mountain against the sky. "Well, I'll go, then," she said. "But if he does come back, Major Doyle, please tell him that I am sorry."

She turned and hurried into the house, and the major nodded darkly.

CHAPTER SIX

Lady Grace reclined listlessly in an easy chair on the verandah of Major Doyle's quarters, while before his office across the way the sentry paced his beat and suppliants came and went. Major Doyle was absolute ruler over an area larger than England—as much a rule as his forces would permit—and, while his adjutant filled out papers and the orderly rushed to and fro, the Indians came to see the Natani. Not his soldiers, not his adjutant, but Whoa Besh himself, the Big Chief.

They were big men, these Navajos, walking lightly in soft red moccasins when they stepped down from their painted horses—men who entered with head up and passed out regally, whether their request had been granted or denied. Always, as they went by, they glanced at her impersonally—at this woman who had come from beyond the Eastern Waters, to whose will even Major Doyle bowed. But Slender Woman ignored them, gazing across the Rio Bravo to where Highest Mountain touched the sky.

For the first time in years she had been balked and
set at naught, and her thoughts were of Silver Hat.

He was a man who had baffled her at every turn,
although how she could not say. She had been
hardly conscious while she dwelt in his mountain
cabin that he had ruled her and dominated her will.
In some deceptive way he had seemed always to
yield—until she had tempted him too far. Then the
faithful Sir Galahad had cast off his cloak and become the primal lover. He had seized her and kissed
her until her senses reeled and she envisioned a new
heaven and earth. But for her, Lady Grace Benedict,
there could be no surrender and she had struck out
blindly—but struck.

The mark of her slender hand was printed in
blood on his cheek while his deep eyes glowed like
fire. He had raised his hand, then dropped it to his
side and spoken words that seared and burned.
There was nothing of reproach for leading him on—
only a biting scorn for all womankind, a hateful con-
tempt for her. Then silence and his broad back,
leading the way through forest fastnesses, and at
the fort his final answer to her blow. He had gone
without a word.

A hot flush of shame mounted to Lady Grace's
brow as she measured the full depth of his hate—a
hate beyond words, finding expression only in silence and a grim return to the wilds. She had called
him her iron man when, with hands that never quiv-
ered, he had plucked the poisonous thorns from her
back, but she had found him a man of steel. He had
dared to flout a Benedict.

As she gazed away into forbidden Kahwestimah,
she remembered how he had thwarted all her plans.

After crossing half a continent to visit the Indians and witness their savage rites, he had denied her the greatest of all. Naked priests with writhing reptiles held fast in their teeth, far mesas given over to pagan gods, ancient plays where First Man and First Woman acted out the beginning of a race. Yet there it lay, this forbidden land of Kahwestimah, and a man was coming down the trail.

She watched him half in reverie as he topped the farthest sand hill and dipped down to the river and crossed. He was an old man with gray hair, but strong and lusty yet, and he ran at a tireless trot. Up the path from the crossing he came on the lope, while his banged hair tossed in the wind. Then he turned in and stood before her, and she awoke from her dreams with a start.

"My . . . boy," he said and grinned expectantly.

"Here, you!" shouted the sentry, running over. "Get out!" He jabbed him with his gun barrel.

"My . . . boy!" demanded the Hopi, holding out his hands, and at the tumult the major strode forth.

"Get out, you old scoundrel!" he ordered. "No, no! Go away! I say go!"

"My . . . boy!" repeated the Indian. Stretching out his neck, he drew his hand across his throat. Then Lady Grace knew him—it was Masawa, Harold's father, and he was asking them to cut off his head.

"Why, Major," she chided, "is Harold still in the guardhouse? I must ask you to release him at once. He had nothing to do with that unfortunate attack . . . and this is his father, I know."

"This is his father," repeated Major Doyle, advancing upon him wearily. "And just to please you . . . and get rid of them both . . . I will order his precious son discharged."

He rapped out a few words to his orderly, and Masawa waited impassively, his snaky eyes shifting from the major to the woman, and then to the distant guardhouse.

"My . . . boy!" he cried as Harold came out. Before the major could prevent him, he had knelt down and seized Lady Grace's hand. She felt a thrill of mingled horror and delight as he bowed and mumbled his thanks, but before she could recover her wits the major booted him away.

"Leave that white woman alone," he commanded sternly, "or by the gods, I'll kill you!"

"Oh, Major!" she protested. "Please don't be so rude. He meant no mischief, I'm sure. It was just his way of expressing his gratitude. . . ."

"I know what he meant," replied the major meaningfully. "That man is a devil in human form. Keep away from him. If . . . you . . . please."

He drew himself up very straight and looked down at her with his gimlet-like eyes, and Lady Grace rose to go.

"Very well," she responded, glancing back at old Masawa, and in the abysmal depths of his snaky black eyes she could sense an inherent malevolence. Devil-worshiper and abductor he might easily be— anything that was evil and lewd. But when she turned to enter the house, he ran after her, while he fumbled in a buckskin pouch.

"He wishes to give you a present," a smooth voice spoke up from behind, and there stood Harold Chasing Butterflies. "He thanks you," he interpreted as the old man jabbered on, "for making them let me out of prison, and he says that Mahcheedo many, many years ago made a prophecy that you would come. So he wants to give you this bead."

He took from Masawa's hand a disk of sky-blue turquoise, worn and polished by centuries of use, but, as she reached out instinctively to receive it, Major Doyle struck the stone away.

"You tell your father," he said to Harold, "that I can read his black heart like a book. Tell him I see the devil's head on that stone. And you, Polinuivah, have gone far enough with this. Now go home . . . and leave her alone."

He reared back his head and looked down his hooked nose at the still-faced, unsmiling Hopi, and Harold Polinuivah stared back.

"If you want to," he challenged, "you can put me in jail. My father says to put him in jail. We are Hopis, or Peace People, and the great prophet said that the White People would be our friends. Everything that is bound to happen, the Hopi priests know it. We love all people who are friends."

"Now, that's enough of that," warned the major impatiently, but Lady Grace was touched.

"I will accept the gift, Harold," she said graciously, and he placed the polished disk in her hand.

"That will bring you good luck," he observed with a smile, "if you wear it around your neck. It is a picture of Masawa, the great Hopi god who rules the world below. When the spirits of dead people go down to that place, he has one word . . . yes or no. He points with his finger from his mouth . . . into

the Good Place or the Bad Place . . . and there they
have to go. My father had a vision. He is Masawa
now. Everything on this earth is his."

He stepped back beaming, and behind him the
old man opened his wide, steel-trap jaws in a smile.
But Lady Grace was looking at the stone. It was
worn almost smooth, but like a shadow on its sur-
face she could see two round eyes, a hollow for a
mouth, the faintest outline of a skull.

"I warned you," spoke the voice of the major in
her ear, "not to take that . . . to leave them alone. You
are playing with witchcraft. They are dangerous
people. That old devil is trying to steal you."

"Oh, now, Major." She laughed. "Of what possible
use is it to speak to me of witchcraft? Am I a child to
believe in sorcery and spells? Of course, I shall accept their gift."

"Very well," he said stiffly, "if you know more
than I do, I will go back and attend to my duties."

He stalked past Masawa with a stern, forbidding
glare and glanced back threateningly at Harold, but
Lady Grace had settled down with an amused, indul-
gent smile, and the Butterfly Chaser was beaming.

"Very old, that stone," he observed, drawing
closer. "Never given to White People before. My father, he say you come to the Snake Dance. He will
let you take a picture."

"Oh, I'd love to." She sighed. "But how can I do it?
Major Doyle will never let me go."

"Ask the major to come, too," he suggested
naïvely. "We have seen how all men love you."

"Why, Harold." She laughed. "You mustn't talk
that way. But still . . . I believe he would. Only how
could we get there? And who would be our guide?"

"I will guide you . . . not cost nothing. Big Snake Dance comes in four days."

"Oh, yes, I know." She nodded and gave a tired sigh.

"My father is chief," he boasted. "What he say, all the Hopis do. I am snake priest, too. I hold snakes in my mouth. Yes, me! No, not afraid!"

"I don't believe you!" she cried incredulously. "Why, you are just back from school."

"I have learned already," he stated complacently, sitting down on his heels on the floor. "You want to hear the story of the Snake Maiden? It never has been told before."

"Yes, Harold," she replied, and laughed softly to herself. Here was romance, close at her hand.

"When people came up from Underworld," he began, "one man, he went to west. He had no clan, no religion, no name. He go west till he come to ocean. There he find track of lady in sand and follow till sun go down. Very lonely . . . he could not sleep. In middle of night he saw fire, out in the ocean, and ladder poles sticking up. Like ladder of kiva, you know . . . underground place where priests keep snakes. Somebody came up this ladder and she had on a white blanket with stripes across the ends . . . dancing blanket, like ladies use. After a while the girl came right up to him."

"Yes, yes." Lady Grace smiled. "Go on."

"He was sitting by fire on sand and he say . . . 'Where you from? Make yourself at home!'

" 'Where are *you* from?' she say, and he laugh.

" 'Right here,' he say. 'This is my home.'

" 'Let's both go to my house,' she say. 'I live out there in the ocean.'

" 'But how will we get there?' he ask. 'I have no way to go.'

" 'I will take care of that,' the lady said, and she take him to edge of water. There he found a big cottonwood log that she had used to cross from kiva and they both stood up on top. The log moved away and it waved and wobbled. It must have been the Big Snake. They rode out there on this Big Snake's back."

He paused impressively and Lady Grace nodded.

"Is this the story of the Snake Dance?" she asked.

"Very, very holy story," he assured her. "Told to me when they made me snake priest. Long story, how she learned him to be snake priest. Maybe someday I tell you more."

"What? The woman taught the man how to handle those dreadful snakes?"

"Learn him everything. How to ketch them, how to sing to them, different kinds of snake clothes to wear. Then, just when sun come up, people have a big race and this boy and this lady win. They run very fast, to ketch sun before it rise away from ground, and something appear before them. It trembled, and all around come rain. That was rainbow, and, when they climbed up on it, it took them quick to sun. It stretch out to the east very far, and where they get off is Kahwestimah. Over there, by Highest Mountain. They have a big Snake Dance and then lots of rain. Lots of corn, lots of beans, lots of melons. That is why we have Snake Dance now."

"Yes, but Harold," she reasoned, "how could that bring the rain?"

"You don't understand," he replied, unruffled. "My people, they know everything. Way down un-

der ground is big snake . . . Pahlulukangwi. He
make big flood, down there. We sing to rattlesnakes,
then let them go back. They tell him, he send big
rain."

"I don't believe it," she scoffed.

"You come . . . we show you," he said. Then he sat
very still, and for the first time she felt their eyes
fixed upon her. Harold's bright and smiling, full of
the light of lusty youth, and old Masawa's strangely
intent. He lay sprawled like a huge rattlesnake
whose lidless eyes are fixed upon some helpless bird
he has struck, and she shuddered and turned away.

"No," she said, rising up, but Harold Polinuivah
only smiled.

"Yes," he said, and with his father he trotted
down to the crossing.

CHAPTER SEVEN

A sultry heaviness lay over old Fort Defiance and that night, as she came out on the verandah, Lady Grace could see the lightning, twinkling and playing over forbidden Kahwestimah. In the morning a soft wind came stealing in from the west, a white cloud came up out of nothing and hovered above Highest Mountain, and the Rio Bravo gleamed like bronze. It was the day they were to start into the west, and, as she gazed across the river, she sighed.

To come so far and brave so much to see the Indians and their rites and then to be turned back from the Snake Dance! Yet Major Doyle was inexorable, her own father had sided against her, and there was nothing but the dead trail west. Covered wagons barely moving as the yoked oxen dragged along, clouds of dust hanging above them like a pall, and all the endless days that must follow would hold the sense of ignominious defeat.

She had donned her buckskin suit to begin their long journey—the silver-bossed tunic, the fringed doeskin skirt, the moccasins with their upturned toes, and the winding leggings gartered with red yarn. For Silver Hat, she knew, would be watching the trail, and he must not think her ungrateful. They were a gift from him, since he had vanished from the fort without waiting for the promised reward, and that day, through his long telescope, he would see for the last time the woman who had claimed his first kiss. What madness had come over her she could not rightly say, since in all things he had been gentle and kind, but with one touch of her hand, like Circe's magic wand, she had transformed him into a lion. Perhaps it was mere pique that the man ever lived who could withstand the allure of her charms so long that he could behold day by day the grace of her perfect form and never even venture a caress. But she had learned to her cost that this Galahad of the plains was a man, and ruled by man's passions. He had seized her with an ardor that had taken away her breath and left her too astonished to resist, until, although she knew she was wrong, she had struck him in the face. A cruel blow, but there was no other way. And then he had gone, without a word.

Lady Grace fixed her eyes on that high, lonely peak beneath which, as she knew, Silver Hat's cabin was hidden. A word from her and Major Doyle's frustrated scouts would know where to seek their man, but as a last, belated loyalty, a single gesture of atonement, she had kept his secret to herself. Desteen had made smoke signals, the scouts had sought his trail, and the major had rebuked her to her face, but she had learned at last the grim reticence of the West, and Silver Hat had not been be-

trayed. As she gazed at the lone peak, a great pang
clutched her heart at the thought of leaving forever.

There was a clatter down by the stables, the
stamping of mules' hoofs, and up along the parade
ground their yellow wagon came trundling, its tires
newly set by the farrier. The stable sergeant saluted
as Lord Benedict appeared, directing the major's
striker with his bags, but, as Doyle came out for the
last farewells, a runner dashed across the ford. He
ran fast, never taking off his moccasins, and Lady
Grace knew him. It was Harold.

"Now what brings that rascal?" grumbled Major
Doyle morosely. But suddenly Lady Grace smiled. A
new light came into her eyes as she watched him
coming closer and she envisioned high adventures,
forgotten dreams. Her lips set in firmer lines, her
heart leaped in her breast, and she felt a wild desire
to go. From the ashes of defeat a new Phoenix bird
arose and she dared once more to hope.

"Oh, Harold," she cried, "have you come to guide
us to the Snake Dance?"

"Yes, lady," he answered gravely. "It is just time, if
we start now."

"Then, Father," she declared, "I'm in favor of going. We could witness the dance and drive back
across the river to join the wagon train below. But I
shall never, never be happy again if we have to give
this up."

Lord Benedict glanced at Doyle, whose eyes were
glittering dangerously, and tugged at his long mus-
tache apologetically. "Well, my dear," he began, "we
have already made Major Doyle so much trouble
that I haven't the face to ask more. But if he will give

us his permission to go, I feel sure we will be quite all right."

The major's narrow eyes grew narrower as he looked at them down his nose and his broad, curved nostrils dilated. He had taken a great deal from this titled Englishman and his willful, golden-haired daughter, and the Irish can be crowded only so far.

"Very well, sir," he said, "you have my permission. But before you start, you will sign a paper to the effect that you have been repeatedly warned . . . that you have rejected my advice already, and have been attacked by these same Indians, but are determined, nevertheless, to go. That will do to show the British Embassy in case any accident should happen . . . and I hope, by the gods, if they beat you up again, they hammer a little sense into your head."

"Well . . . *ahem*," began Lord Benedict, dropping his glasses to the end of their string, "this is rather straight talk, don't you think?"

"Yes, and I mean every word of it," returned the major. "So make up your minds . . . yes or no."

His lordship adjusted his glasses and glanced at his daughter. "Well, in that case," he said, "we will go."

"Yes, indeed!" chimed in Lady Grace.

"Go it is," responded the major. "And I'll go right along with you, and take a full troop of cavalry. I've been fooling with old Masawa long enough . . . and with his smooth-tongued, educated son. So listen to me, Polinuivah, and don't you forget this. I have orders from Washington to put down this woman stealing at any cost, and I know more about it than you think. You have had your last chance on this al-

ibi business, and, if a hair of her head is touched, I'll
level Yahoya to the ground."

"Yes, sir," answered Harold pertly. "It is just time
to see the dance, if we start."

"We will start," said Doyle, "when I give the order. And just to make my precaution complete, I'll
take along the Navajo scouts."

"Yes, sir," replied Polinuivah, suddenly losing his
smile. "But maybeso that will make trouble. Hopi
people don't like it to have Navajos come to
dances."

"No, but I do, Harold," said the major, and hurried off to assemble his troops.

"Well, my dear"—Lord Benedict smiled—"this is
so sudden, as the widow said when her man proposed, but perfectly satisfactory to me. I have felt all
along that the major's absurd prejudice was depriv-
ing us of the experience of a lifetime, and, of course,
if he wishes to make this great show of strength, our
safety is doubly assured. It is quite fortunate, all
around, but just to allay Doyle's fears, may I ask you
to be very discreet?"

"Yes, *Pater*,"—she smiled back—"the very picture
of discretion. I shall never leave your side. But I still
fail to see what there is about poor Harold that
makes all these soldiers hate him."

"I am educated," spoke up Harold. "I am smart,
like they are. Soldiers like all Indians to be afraid.
But my father is great prophet. He is not afraid of
soldiers. No, not if they cut off his head."

"But why is it, Harold," inquired Lord Benedict,
"that you are blamed for stealing those women?
That seems to be the grievance of Major Doyle
against you, and I must confess it influenced me."

"Kahwestimah bad country," confessed Polinuivah. "Bad people live by Highest Mountain. Bad Paiute, bad Navajo, bad white man . . . they blame all their stealing on us."

"Oh, indeed!" observed Lord Benedict. "You never mentioned the white men before. Is it they who steal the women?"

Harold stirred uneasily and glanced about for some escape. "All steal 'em," he said, smiling darkly, "and try to put blame on Hopis. But you look out at Snake Dance . . . sometimes bad white man come. Crying Man, we call him, because tears run down his face. He lives where boat crosses river."

"Ah, the ferry on the Colorado. But who is this man with the rheumy eyes? Is he an outlaw, such as we read of?"

"Same kind," agreed Harold, brightening up. "Steal horses from Mormons and sell them to Indians. Steal from Indians and sell to other Mormons. Steal cattle from everybody . . . cowboys come and have big fight. He kill them . . . kill everybody. Then he cry."

"You mean he weeps, like a woman?"

"No. No weep . . . just have tears run down. All time he laugh, very loud."

"My word!" exclaimed his lordship, looking over at his daughter. "We've rather let ourselves in for it, what? If I'd known of these border outlaws . . ."

"No, *Pater*," she replied firmly, "it's too late now. But we must be very careful not to separate from the soldiers. And Harold, don't be so saucy to Major Doyle. We are dependent upon his good will."

"Oh, that's all right," answered Harold easily. "He is mad at me already. Long time ago they take me from my people and make me go to school. They put my father in prison. But he is great prophet . . . knows all that will happen . . . so he let me go away. Now, when I come back, the major, he is mad because I am not a fool. I can read. I know the laws. That is why I only laugh when he say he will tear down Yahoya." He chuckled indulgently and gazed far away, out the trail that led to Kahwestimah. "I am not afraid of nothing," he said. "My father knows all that will happen."

"Well, well," commented Lord Benedict, "a strange power, I'm sure. But did I understand you, Harold, to say some time ago that he knew my daughter would come?"

"He knows everything," replied Polinuivah serenely. "And everywhere he go he makes come lots of rain. Lots of Hopi come to live there. They raise lots of corn, lots of melons, lots of beans. Other Hopis have nothing . . . starve. Long time ago he live at Oraibi. Bear clan, they run that town. But he had a vision that all this world is his, so Bear Chief drove him away. Now Oraibi is nothing . . . all houses falling down. No rain there, because snake clan move away."

"So that is the secret of his power," marveled Lord Benedict. "I foresee, Grace dear, this will be very interesting. Quite the greatest of all our adventures. But what is it? What are you thinking of?"

"I was wondering," she said, "about Silver Hat. He will not know where we have gone."

"Not know?" he repeated, staring. "And what difference will that make, my dear?"

"I . . . I have a feeling," she confessed, "he will be watching for us to pass. And we owe him a great deal, you know."

"Do you wish to change our plans?" he asked. "It is not too late, you know."

"Well, perhaps . . . ," she began, but Harold cut her short.

"He is no good!" he stated vindictively, and suddenly her proud head went up.

"Kindly speak when you are spoken to," she said. "I was talking to my father."

"He is bad man!" burst out Harold. "He tells lies about my people."

"Here, here!" exclaimed Lord Benedict, pushing him roughly back. "We must have none of this, young man. Please hold your tongue in the presence of your betters. You are most unmannerly before my daughter."

"If he comes to Yahoya," said Polinuivah slowly, "my people will kill him . . . sure."

He stood facing them, boldly, and after a moment of startled silence, the Englishman drew his daughter aside. "Shall we turn back?" he asked under his breath. "I fear he will make us more trouble."

Lady Grace glanced at Harold, who stood watching her confidently, and at the long line of soldiers clattering out. Then she let her eyes wander out the winding trail that led across the Bravo to Kahwestimah—to the smoothly molded sand hills, red as blood, and Highest Mountain beckoning her on.

"No," she said. "I am going to cross that river."

And Harold Chasing Butterflies smiled.

CHAPTER EIGHT

The storm clouds were rushing up, whirling dust and sand before them, when Lady Grace made her crossing of the Rio Bravo. There was a clatter over the smooth rocks, a splash of red mud followed by a shower of turbid water that marred the polish of the yellow spring wagon. The Navajo scouts on horse-back plied their quirts on the mules to keep them moving. The river rose dangerously, flowing over the submerged axles and flooding the box in a wave when the wagon struck a deep pothole, until with a wild scramble the mules pulled free and tugged the wagon up the opposite bank. Although her white skirt was spoiled, Lady Grace looked out, laughing, and the grim-faced Navajos laughed back. Here was something to talk about in the hogans of their people—of this woman, so strangely beautiful, who ruled all the White People, making them take her where she would. And the stories were true about this man from beyond the Eastern Ocean. He must be a great chief in his own country, for to escort them to the Snake Dance one hundred armed soldiers were sent, besides these Navajo scouts.

They had entered Kahwestimah, the mystic first home of the Hopis, and for what was left of the day they toiled west in the teeth of a growing sandstorm while troopers tied their picket ropes to the tongue of the wagon to help the dispirited mules. But at dusk the wind ceased and they camped by a deep spring, where a stairway went down into the ground. Armed herders took out the horses to graze during the night, supper was cooked and beds made down, and then on a low butte a fire flared up, and Desteen, the old medicine man, stood beside it. He raised his blanket and lowered it quickly, sending mysterious winks of light to the south, and Lady Grace watched him curiously.

"To whom is he signaling?" she asked the major.

"To Silver Hat, maybe," he answered at last with a grunt. "He's down in those mountains somewhere."

"Oh, wouldn't it be jolly if he'd join us!" she cried.

The major grunted again. "He won't answer," he replied. "The best scout I've got."

Lady Grace felt the reproof. To avoid her, Silver Hat had fled into the wilderness, refusing to answer even his grandfather, Desteen. And every day that she remained, holding the troops as her escort, the chances of his return dwindled away. But not for all the world, now she had crossed into Kahwestimah, would she give up seeing the Snake Dance. The snakes were all gathered, and, in the kivas of Yahoya, priests and neophytes lingered over them with prayers.

On the second of the nine days they proceeded to the north, following up every snake track, striking the bushes with their sticks, digging out those that darted down holes. The next day they went west, then south and east, and on the fifth day all ways at once. Now the snakes were kept in tightly closed jars, awaiting the final morning when they would be bathed and sung to as gods. All this Harold had told her, now sitting familiarly beside her in spite of her father's hints, and in the morning, when they roused up, he stood before them, panting, his black hair tangled by the wind.

"Why, Harold," she exclaimed from her boudoir in the wagon, "where have you been so early?"

"To Yahoya," he responded. "My father is expecting you. The dance is tomorrow afternoon."

"Is it so near?" inquired her father, rising up to look.

"Forty miles," said Polinuivah.

"And do you mean to say," demanded Lord Benedict, "that you have been there and back so soon?"

"Run all night," answered Harold. "Navajos call me *jedih* . . . that means Antelope."

"My word," ejaculated Benedict, "this is most extraordinary. I must make a note for our book. But run along now, while we dress and have breakfast."

Reluctantly the Hopi walked off.

Bugles blew, saluting the sun, and the horse herd came in. The tough mules were harnessed again, and then, heading north, they rattled along over hard ground while smooth blue buttes rose before them. They were entering the fairyland of the Painted Desert, where every cliff and wash was overlaid with colors that almost dazzled the eye. There were cinnamon-brown hills like huge cakes of gingerbread and lesser mounds that resembled blue icings, and then in pure tones black and white, red and green, and high cliffs yellow as gold.

The sun rose and fell as if Grandmother, the Hopi Spider Woman, was indeed speeding their course with her web, and then, from the summit of a rainbow-hued cliff, they beheld the Red Mesa, Yahoya. It rose against the sky, straight-topped and straight-walled, a citadel in the desert, the last retreat of an ancient people who cried—"Peace!"—where there was no peace. Above it like a crown rose a billowy white cloud, black and threatening at its base.

"See the rain!" exclaimed Harold, pausing in awe from running alongside the wagon. "You know what makes it come? Snake priests . . . saying prayers!"

They glanced at him, standing at gaze, his dark eyes strangely luminous, and Lady Grace turned away. He had changed since that day when, against her will, he had persuaded her to come to Kahwestimah. He had been calm and smiling then, assured and yet not bold, but now, viewing the magic of his people, he swelled with savage arrogance.

"You look!" he challenged. "Only rain on our mesa. All rest of country dry. You think the White People know how to do that? What we care you bring all these soldiers?" He waved his hand contemptuously at the double column of cavalrymen, and Lord Benedict ventured a reproof.

"In my country," he stated, "it rains a great deal. The grass is always green. But our priests claim no credit for a purely natural phenomenon. We believe that God sends the rain."

"Huh!" Harold laughed. "He don't send it out

here. Government sent out one missionary for be Indian farmer . . . learn Hopis how they ought to grow corn . . . and he planted big field out on plain. My father, he plant 'nother field and say to this White People . . . 'All right, now, you pray for rain. You pray to White People's God. I pray to Hopi gods. You pray to make rain on your field.'" He paused, showing his white teeth in a broad, triumphant grin. "You think that missionary raise corn? His field dry up. He 'shamed . . . go away. But my father, he have lot of corn!"

He trotted on chuckling, shaking out his mane of hair, and Lord Benedict grumbled: "My word, what cheek the beggar has. I'll be glad when we see the last of him. But we must indulge him, my dear, until after the ceremony. It will really be worth the price. But think of his father, deluding the people by claiming to make it rain."

"Masawa had a strange look," answered Lady Grace. "I would not care to trust him too far. But, surely, with all these soldiers to protect us . . . I wish I had not accepted his bead." She drew out the polished turquoise and gazed at it ruefully. "Do you think they really worship devils?"

"Undoubtedly," returned her father easily. "In fact, all savages do. But that they give them any power, whether for good or evil, is something I very much question."

She looked again at the deep, skull-like eyes, the grinning mouth, the straight line for a nose, and shuddered as she put it away. With that line and three holes, the barbaric etcher had imparted a look of hate. There was a fantastic leer, almost obscene in its stark wickedness, that gave her a chill of fear, and yet, since old Masawa had given it as a present, she dared not throw it away.

As they drove closer to Yahoya and saw the strange path that led up its sheer red wall, she wondered if all was well. It followed up the crest of a huge eddy of sand that the west wind had piled against its base, and to span the last reach a long ladder had been reared that could be hauled up or thrown down at will. But for this one trail, Red Mesa was an island in a land that reeked with hate.

When the soldiers rode in to the walled-up spring that seeped out of the drifted sand, naked children swarmed the cliff, peering fearfully down until their mothers ran and snatched them back. All night from their camp they could hear excited voices and the town crier, shouting from the house tops, and the next morning, when Harold came down, there was a wild excitation in his eyes.

"You stay here," he ordered, "until dance this afternoon. Snake people have ceremonies and wash snakes down in kiva and they don't want soldiers to come up. No soldiers, no Navajos . . . just you and me. My father is mad at soldiers."

"What's that?" demanded Lord Benedict indignantly. "You say no soldiers may come up? Why, that is exactly contrary to Major Doyle's orders. He insists that my daughter shall be guarded."

"No. Cannot see dance, then," returned Harold with finality. "Snake priests have big council, then send me to tell you. No soldiers can come up on rock."

"And why not?" asked Lady Grace.

"People think," explained Polinuivah, "that soldiers come to tear down houses. What for did they bring all those picks? Hopi women cry all night and hide children in cellars. They think soldiers will take them to school."

"Why, no, Harold," she protested, "you know, as well as I do, why Major Doyle brought all these men. And I will never set foot on that mesa unless they are permitted to follow."

"No? Not come?" cried Harold in dismay. "Not climb up to see the great Snake Dance? This is first time I dance and carry snakes in mouth. You come, I show you everything."

"Never," she declared. "Unless the soldiers accompany us. You have not kept your word, Polinuivah."

"And I dare say," put in her father, "when the major hears of this, you will find yourself called to account. It was distinctly understood we should have free access to your village and the privilege of taking photographs. Because of your bad name in connection with these emigrant trains, Major Doyle insists upon accompanying us."

"All a lie!" flared up Harold. "Told by Silver Hat to hurt my people. Hopitu means Peace People. We love all who are friends. But he is bad man . . . he is Navajo!"

He spat out the word vindictively, then fell silent as Major Doyle appeared.

"Well," he inquired mildly, "what seems to be the trouble this morning? Let nobody tell you the Hopis are Peace People. They're the most quarrelsome varmints in the world."

"Why," exclaimed his lordship, "after bringing us clear out here, he has the effrontery to inform us that no soldiers can go up on top! And unless my daughter and I will consent to go alone, we cannot see the dance."

"People are all afraid you will tear down houses," interposed Polinuivah hurriedly. "They ask why soldiers bring picks. But if lady and I go up, I will take her down in kiva . . . show her everything. Only mister cannot take any pictures."

"But you gave me your word . . . ," began Benedict indignantly.

Major Doyle laughed to himself and said: "A Hopi will tell you anything to gain his purpose. I've had some experience. But before I'd allow my daughter to go down into that kiva, I would ask myself . . . what is that purpose?"

"You mean, sir," demanded Lord Benedict, "they are plotting to steal Grace? If I believed that for an instant, I should immediately leave the country and turn this scamp over to the authorities."

"Oh, no! No, sir!" protested Harold, breaking in. "My people think this lady is a god. Long time ago prophet Mahcheedo say she is coming. It is only the soldiers we don't like."

"Well, the soldiers are here," spoke up Major Doyle. "And wherever she goes, they go. So make up your mind, right now, whether you will let her see the dance."

"Yes, yes. She can see!" cried Polinuivah in a panic. "Prophet say she must see the Snake Dance. Everything that is bound to happen he knew long ago. So all right, everybody come up."

"And will I be permitted to take photographs?" inquired his lordship. "That was part of your promise, you know."

"Yes, can take pictures," assented Harold, beaming amiably. "But lots of snakes on ground. You take from my house top. Snake Dance is right below."

"Agreed, then," responded Benedict. "But remember this, young man. No welshing . . . you must keep your word."

"Yes . . . always do," said Harold Chasing Butterflies.

The major laughed cynically.

CHAPTER NINE

The edge of Red Mesa was crowded with Hopis, craning their necks, almost toppling to a fall, when hand over hand, with a confident smile, Lady Grace climbed up the steep ladder. Major Doyle and two troopers, armed with pistols and carbines, led the way and stood at the top, while behind her, lugging his camera, Lord Benedict came on slowly, with more soldiers bringing up the rear. Then followed the Navajo scouts, entering the stronghold of their enemies with taunting, triumphant leers, eager to see the great Snake Dance of the Monkey People.

She paused at the last rung, eying the bobbing heads above her, whose movements made them almost seem like monkeys, and one boyish face, thrust out beyond the rest, caused her to flinch and loosen her hold. In the impish stare of his beady black eyes, the twisted lips and matted hair there was something that repelled her—yet why she could not tell, more than that she had seen him before. She clutched at the ladder as the ever-watchful major lay a steadying hand on her arm. Then she glanced up, smiling wanly, and stepped out on the ancient rock, worn deep by the passage of many feet.

"You must be careful," he warned. "These people are not friendly. Come directly with me and I will clear the chief's house top and get you out of this crowd."

"I . . . I don't mind," she protested. "Only there was one face among them . . ."

"That you recognized?" prompted Major Doyle.

"Why . . . I seemed to," she answered. "And yet I can't remember where it was I have seen it before. And that picture on the cliff. Didn't you notice it when we came up? It was the same as the face on my turquoise."

"That's the picture of the devil they worship," he said. "I hope you haven't worn that bead? Well, keep it out of sight. These people are on an orgy . . . there's no telling what may happen."

He rapped out an order and with military brusqueness the soldiers made way before them. Women and children were thrust aside and old men jostled until at last they helped her up a ladder and she stood on a broad, flat roof.

"Are you unwell?" inquired the major solicitously, and suddenly she clutched at his arm.

"I don't know why it is," she confessed, "but really I seem quite shaken. It must have been that face that I saw in the crowd . . . and they're not as I expected at all. Not the least like handsome Harold. They're so filthy and ragged and . . . well, repulsive. Like beggars that I have seen."

"Perhaps," he suggested quietly, "they're like the beggars who attacked your wagon."

Then as he felt her reel, he supported her and motioned his orderly for a folding chair.

"It's all right," he said. "There's no danger at all. I was hoping, if you came, that you might recognize one of those rascals. We knew they were Hopis all the time."

"But, Major," she protested, "was it right to let me come, then?"

"Well, really, Miss Benedict," he returned, "I had very little choice in the matter. It was against my protest that you made this trip. But now that you're here, we'll see it through."

"And Harold?" she quavered. "Was he really behind it? Did he send those filthy beggars to attack me?"

"We believe so," replied the major impersonally.

"Then he ought to be arrested!" she cried.

"Not so loud." He frowned. "These Hopis are all ears, and some of them have been to school. But after the dance is over, if all goes well, we will take him back to the fort."

"You don't mean that the Hopis would resist?"

"We came prepared for that," he answered grimly. "But they are playing a desperate game. What it is I do not know, but they are determined at any cost to get you up on that mesa."

"This is terrible," she declared, rising up as her father appeared. "But please say nothing to *Pater*. His heart is set upon securing these photographs. It is enough that I should understand."

She smiled up at the major, who nodded assent and hurried off to post his men, and then, quite composed, Lady Grace looked about at the scene that lay before them. They were standing upon the first terrace of a three-storied house that rose above them in laddered walls, while in the open floor behind them a single narrow hatchway gave access to the storeroom below. There were no doors on the ground floor, to lend aid to treachery, and the soldiers were clearing the house.

In the plaza below a double line of troopers had marched in and taken possession of the square. Guards were posted at each entrance, and along the sheer edge of the precipice the Navajo scouts stood fearlessly. Squads of men hurried to and fro, searching houses, removing ladders, regardless of shrill Hopi protests, until at last, in a sudden panic, the women seized their children and disappeared into their storage rooms like rats. But relentlessly Major Doyle routed them out until the house of the snake chief was safe. Then, bounding up the ladder that led down through the hatchway, he appeared before Lord Benedict.

"The house is empty," he announced, "as I know from my own inspection. Now I shall post a heavy guard on every floor and leave you in sole possession. Is that satisfactory to you both?"

"Quite, quite," replied his lordship. "If you consider it necessary. But I fear, Major Doyle, in your praiseworthy zeal, you have quite disrupted our Snake Dance. All the natives have fled except this one old man who is tending the reptiles in that booth. . . ."

"They'll be back," broke in the major. "These are only the common people. The snake priests are down in their kiva. But do not forget . . . you have been placed in my charge. It is my first duty to see that you are safe."

"Then, if that is your sole purpose," responded Benedict testily, "allow me to commend your industry. Now perhaps you will announce to the snake priests that I am ready for the dance to begin. The hour is getting late, and with these clouds rushing up I am afraid I shall lose my light. Oh, and ask Polinuivah to request the town crier to tell all the people to return."

"Very well," returned the major, hurrying off, and Lord Benedict stamped his foot in a rage.

"Of all the crass impudence . . . ," he began, but his daughter lay her hand on his lips.

"No, Father," she said, "he is only doing his duty. And if we knew what he knows about the treachery of these creatures, I am sure we would wish to thank him."

"What, what," he exclaimed, clutching her arm, "have you had some unpleasant experience? My dear child, your cheeks are quite pale. What is it that has changed you so?"

"I saw a face, in the crowd," she began, ". . . but this is not the time to explain. We have come so far to get your photographs that nothing must interfere."

"Very well," he replied, reaching hastily for his tripod. "I must set up my camera at once. But if anything should happen to threaten your safety . . ."

"Nothing will happen," she said. "We are perfectly safe now. But I have just come to realize that but for Major Doyle, we should be in serious peril."

"I never trusted that Polinuivah," he answered absently, working busily with his lens and black box, and then abruptly he ducked under his focusing cloth and she glanced about, biting her lip.

The people came swarming back as the crier bellowed his call, popping up unexpectedly from every roof and cellar, hurrying in to get a place in the plaza, and it seemed as they stood waiting that every eye in that audience was fixed unblinkingly on her. But the long-expected dancers failed to appear and at last Major Doyle came back.

"The snake priests," he announced, "have refused to begin the dance until every soldier has left their chief's house. That Masawa is a sorehead and he understands his advantage . . . he knows you came to see the dance."

"Not only to see it . . . to photograph it, my dear Major," Lord Benedict responded. "And how can that be done without light? In another half hour, with these clouds in the west, I shall be unable to expose a plate. So please clear the house at once and beg the chief to proceed."

"Very well," returned Doyle reluctantly, "but kindly remain in plain sight from the ground. I suspect . . ."

"Yes, yes," sputtered the Englishman, "but please tell them immediately. My daughter and I are quite safe."

He strode about impatiently, glancing now at the rolling clouds and now at the empty plaza, until suddenly from a darkened kiva a line of priests emerged, walking quietly, their faces grave. Each was stripped to the waist, their bronze bodies painted in white, and, as they marched ceremoniously into the square, they shook rattles that sounded like a snake. It was the antelope priests, brother actors of the snake clan, and Lord Benedict sprang into action. Dodging under his black focusing cloth he racked out his long bellows and opened his lens up wide. Then, thrusting in his plate holder, he stepped aside and released his shutter, reversed his holder, and shot again.

"Excellent. Excellent," he whispered. "Now, if only the snake priests would appear."

But there was no breaking or hurrying of the ancient ritual that had come down unchanged through the centuries. Four times with measured strides the antelope priests paced the entire circumference of the square, and each time, as they passed the *kisi*, they stamped upon a broad plank. In a deep hole beneath it, almost hidden by cottonwood boughs, lay a great buckskin sack full of the rattlesnakes that were to convey the Hopis' prayers to the Water God. To Pahlulukangwi, the Plumed Serpent of the Underworld, who by turning over could release the flood.

They sprinkled sacred meal ceremonially and lined up with their backs to the chief's house, on either side of the *kisi*. Then from the entrance there came a sound of rattling, produced by many deer toes crashing in unison against empty tortoise shells, and into the plaza, like warriors going into battle, the snake priests came stalking, on the rampage. They were big men, broad-shouldered and burly, and, as they passed the Navajo scouts, they buffeted them angrily aside.

Straight down the line they passed, as if their enemies did not exist, and at the end they swung back and paced past the *kisi*, stamping loudly on the plank, the entrance to the Underworld, beneath which a man tended the snakes. Their naked bodies were painted black, their mouths broadened with daubs of white, and across the dark field of their dancing skirts an arrow point of lightning struck. Red feathers crowned their heads, turquoise necklaces hung strand on strand, and, sign of their calling, each carried a feathered snake whip to fend off the blows of their pets. Gorgeous yellow and red fox skins hung behind them as they trod, and, after circling four times, they lined up before the *kisi*, facing their fellows of the antelope clan.

The flat rattles vibrated like the tails of angry snakes, and, out of the silence like the thunder of a storm, a low and solemn chant began. So tremendous was the effect of this upwelling of sonorous sound that even Lord Benedict stood awed. The dancers swayed as if swept by passing winds, then, as the chorus rose to its greatest height and came to a deep-voiced end, they broke up in parties of three. In the lead, gray-haired Masawa reached into the bower and put a long snake in his mouth. His protector walked behind him, one hand over his shoulder to fend off the vicious head, while in their rear the watchful gatherer followed closely, to pick up the snake if dropped.

The second leader reached in and snatched out a writhing reptile that struggled in vain to bite him, but always the stiff feathers of the snake whip intervened, and they strode on, unshaken by the assault. On the roof Lady Grace was almost in a trance at the barbarous sublimity of the scene, while trio after trio in quick succession received their snake and marched on sedately. Except for the quick thrusts of the snake whip and the shake of some endangered head, there was nothing to suggest that each man in his mouth carried a messenger of sudden death,

and, last of all, in his place at the end, came Harold
Polinuivah, the neophyte.

He reached in confidently and brought forth a
squirming rattlesnake. He balanced it in his hand,
then with the greatest composure closed his teeth
down on the body near the neck. He straightened
up and marched off proudly, an Indian of the
Indians—a barbarian for all his schooling—the son
of old Masawa, the snake chief. Lady Grace drew
back, clutching her hands in apprehension as the
angry snake writhed to strike, but always between
his fangs and the smiling countenance the fending
snake whip was thrust. They passed on tri-
umphantly, and, for the first time since the dance
began, she glanced about at the crowd.

They stood as in a spell, Hopis and Navajos alike,
watching the spectacle with frightened eyes, and,
each time a carried snake was dropped, they surged
back in a frantic stampede. The leaders of the dance
had completed their first circuit and let their snakes
fall to the ground, while behind, watching vigilantly
but delaying to pick them up, the gatherers hovered
over them. Some rattlesnakes coiled viciously and
struck back at the brushing whip, and, as one of
these straightened out and darted for the cliff edge,
the Navajo scouts broke and fled. Only one man
stood his ground, and, as Grace looked again, she
recognized him as Silver Hat.

He remained unmoved as a warning yell went up
and the snake threw a coil at his feet, then with a
deft flip of his moccasin he kicked it away, and the
gatherer snatched it up. They bristled at each other
angrily, for a messenger to Pahlulukangwi had been

struck, and the snake priest raised his hand, but, as Silver Hat started toward him, he turned in his tracks and took his place in the dance. The Navajos laughed and came trooping back to watch, and Silver Hat glanced up at Lady Grace.

There was something in his eyes that she did not understand—perhaps he was angry at the snake gatherer—but, after one look, he turned away and the tumult among the dancers waxed furious. There were rattlesnakes everywhere, some writhing to escape, some fighting angrily back, and more than one carrier was forced to drop his burden to keep from being bit. Each gatherer had a handful of reptiles, some harmless, some swelling with venom, and at a signal that the snake bag was empty, they bore them to the end of the square.

Now the snake maidens appeared, clad in striped white dancing blankets to sprinkle the snake messengers with sacred meal, and, as a circle was drawn, they were all hurled into it while the priests gathered closely about them. Old Masawa shouted an order, certain men rushed to the front, and then the final act began. First Harold Polinuivah snatched up a double handful of reptiles and darted off toward the ladder down the cliff. Another priest went bounding away to the north, dropping snakes right and left among the crowd. Then, like devils out of hell, the remaining snake priests charged, and soldiers and scouts alike stampeded.

There were rattlesnakes everywhere, writhing and striking out waspishly, and, in a pandemonium of yells and curses, Lady Grace's soldier guard broke and fled. From his vantage ground on the roof Lord Benedict was working madly to photograph this last wild scene, and, while his daughter stood beside him to hand him his plate holder, he ducked under his black focusing cloth. For a moment he racked the lens back and forth, and, when he came out, she was gone. Only the plate holder, halfway to the hatchway, marked the direction in which she had vanished.

CHAPTER TEN

The first man on the roof in the mad search for Lady Grace was Major Doyle, and within a minute after the panic he had his troopers back at their posts. At double quick, a cordon of soldiers was thrown about the town with orders to let no one out. Then, down into the storeroom of the snake chief's house, they poured like ants into a hole. Matches were scratched, cornhusks fired and held on high, and old timbers uprooted by main strength, but nowhere could the lady be found. She had disappeared down the hatchway, leaving nothing but a devil's head turquoise to show she had ever been there.

"Throw out all that corn!" ordered the major. "Clear the place . . . she's hidden here somewhere. Either that or there's a door that leads out. The girl has been kidnapped, that is plain."

"But why?" clamored Lord Benedict frantically. "Why should they want to take my daughter away? If it's ransom they wish, I will accede to it willingly, but I simply can't understand."

"For the same reason," replied the major, "that the other women were taken. I warned you from the first to keep out of Kahwestimah and I've got your signature to prove it, but it's too late to discuss that now. We must search this town from top to bottom and examine every kiva. The snake priests were behind this . . . old Masawa and Harold. And when I catch them. . . ."

He paused as a loud boom of thunder made the earth quake beneath their feet. Then, on the dirt roof above them, the rain came sluicing down with the fierce, torrential sweep of a flood. Pahlulukangwin, the Plumed Serpent of the Underworld, had heard the prayers of his priests, and suddenly earth and sky were obscured—in such darkness that the coming of night passed unnoticed. Beaten back by rain and wind the soldiers strove heroically to guard every exit from the town, but when the storm had passed and they went from house to house, not a snake priest, not a man could be found. They had slipped away in the protecting darkness to escape the wrath of Major Doyle, leaving their women and children to the mercy of the *Bohanas*, whose weakness their prophets had foretold. Only against those who fought back would the white men raise their hands. Even their enemies were safe if they but bared their breasts and invited the fatal thrust. So the wily ones slunk away into the night and in the storeroom the major's men toiled on.

Tiers of corn were yanked down and heaved out into the wet; old masks and strange idols followed after them, but although they dug deeper and deeper into the rubbish of centuries, no hiding place, no passageway could be found.

"Bring up the picks!" ordered the major impatiently, but while he was still fretting and fuming, Silver Hat came struggling down the ladder. His buckskin suit was soaked, his big hat spilled out water, but in one hand, firmly gripped by the neck, he bore old Masawa himself.

"By the gods!" exulted Doyle. "So you caught the damned scoundrel! Bring him down here . . . I want to talk to him."

He drew himself up arrogantly, canting his fighting head back until his nose thrust out like a beak, but when the snake chief beheld him, he spat like a cat and tried to bite Silver Hat's hand.

"Where did you find the old rascal?" the major asked.

"Down at the foot of the mesa, heading west. I tried to catch Harold, when he came down the ladder, but he got away in the storm. I was coming back around the trail when Masawa ran right into me."

"Good enough," commended Doyle. "Now we've got something to work on. You tell him," he went on, "to surrender that woman, or I'll take it out of his hide. Make it strong . . . I mean what I say."

Masawa stood glowering as, in labored Hopi, the scout repeated the threat. Then with a vindictive twist, he thrust out his turtle neck and ran his hand across his throat. "Cut my head off!" he challenged. "Kill me!"

"You tell him," yelled the major, "that I'll do just that if he doesn't bring back this girl! He knows where she is and I want her back, unharmed. Otherwise, I'll tear down the town and break his damned neck to boot."

"No!" returned the old chief scornfully. "The Hopis

are not afraid. The Big Chief at Washington will punish you if your soldiers tear down my house."

"Tell him to wait," shrilled the major, "till my men come back with those picks! I'll show him that I'm the chief here. See what you can do with him, Silver Hat."

The scout nodded and took off his big sombrero with the Mexican eagle on the side.

"You see this?" he asked in Hopi, placing his finger on the silver ornament. "That is a present to me from Washington. That shows what my orders are. I am to be like the American eagle and catch the snakes in my claws. Washington has given me orders to kill every snake priest that tries to steal a woman."

He stood eying the old man sternly, and then he spoke again.

"You are old," he said, "but your heart is bad. You talk like a snake, with two tongues. I know you should be killed, but I do not fight old men. I will save this for your son."

He drew out his long, polished hunting knife and ran his finger along the keen edge, and for the first time Masawa quailed.

"He is the one," went on Silver Hat, "who has been stealing these white women, but we Navajos know how to find him. I will follow him up and kill him, as sure as this knife cuts, unless he brings back that girl."

"My boy has done nothing . . . ," protested Masawa weakly, but Silver Hat cut him short.

"I know what he has done," he said. "Will you give up the girl . . . or shall I kill him?"

The old man glanced around at the hard-eyed men and at last he bowed his head. "If any bad people have stolen her," he said, "I will see that the woman is returned."

"She was taken into this room," accused Major Doyle hotly. "Tell him to show us where she is hid."

Masawa listened sullenly as the charge was interpreted, and suddenly his head went up. "No!" he answered defiantly.

"Then tell him," went on Doyle, "that I will tear down his house. And if I find a door, I will kill him."

"Just a moment!" broke in Lord Benedict, who had been listening anxiously. "It seems to me that, as the father of Lady Grace, I should have the final word. It is very evident that your threats of violence have had no effect on this fanatic. So, before you deliver this ultimatum, I should like to make him an offer. I will give him her weight in gold for my daughter, if she is returned at once and unharmed."

Silver Hat glanced at the major, who pursed his lips grimly.

"Have you got the gold?" he inquired.

"I have, sir," returned Lord Benedict, "and as an earnest of my intentions I will ask you to show him this."

He unbuckled a money belt concealed beneath his jacket and shook out a handful of gold coins.

Silver Hat took the money and stood looking at Masawa, who regarded him with a leering smile. Then he interpreted slowly, expounding the value of the gold, and waited for an answer. The old man hefted the sovereigns, protesting against their weight, looking them over with skeptical eyes.

"I want silver," he said at last. "He is trying to cheat me. I have never seen money like this."

"It is good," replied Silver Hat, "and every piece will buy five silver dollars."

There was a clatter above as Masawa continued

his objections, and down the hatchway, one after the other, great armfuls of picks were passed.

"Tell him to make up his mind," said the major.

But still the haggling went on. A dozen times the men seized their picks and attacked the foundations of his house and each time he pretended to yield. With the art of a diplomat he played the father love of the Englishman against the stern impatience of the soldier, but, as the pale light of dawn came down through the hatchway he threw all pretense aside.

"No!" he snarled, hurling the sovereigns on the floor.

Major Doyle leaped up, cursing. "Tear the house down!" he ordered. "He's made fools of us long enough. Dig up the floor first and, by the gods, if I find a passageway . . ."

They dug while, bound fast, Masawa looked on with a grin that grew wider with the hours, but toward noon a hollow sound revealed a space beneath a rock and soon a narrow passageway was found. It followed a natural fissure in the sandstone of the cliff, and, as the searchers went down, they came to a stairway that led to the foot of the mesa. Major Doyle took one look at the rain-soaked sand and turned back with a curse. Lady Grace had been carried away the night before and every track was obliterated by the storm.

CHAPTER ELEVEN

Without a word to Masawa, Major Doyle summoned every man, and swiftly and methodically, while the Hopi women wailed, he leveled his house to the ground. Stone after stone was hurled over the cliff, the timbers were piled up and burned, but through it all the old snake chief sat unmoved, muttering prayers to his pagan gods. Lord Benedict watched him hopefully, furtively flashing his golden sovereigns, but when the third story came down with a roar, he turned and walked away. All his dreams had come to nothing, his daughter was lost, and Major Doyle's revenge left him cold.

As he strode along the cliff, looking off across the desert, he met Silver Hat coming up the ladder. He was followed by Desteen, the old Navajo medicine man, and his lordship stopped short and spoke.

"Silver Hat," he began, "you must know a father's feelings at seeing his daughter stolen. I am sure you would help me if you could. But would it be any inducement if I offered to you the reward this old chief has spurned? I mean . . . my daughter's weight in gold. You cannot imagine how gladly I would pay to have her safely back in my arms. Only find her and the gold is yours."

"Nope," responded Silver Hat, "you don't need to pay. The money is nothing to me."

"Then help me out of kindness . . . for my daughter's sake. You have such a knowledge of Indians and their ways . . . is there no way in which they might assist?"

"Why . . . yes," returned Silver Hat. "Desteen is a hand-shaker. If you give him five dollars, he might sing to Tinlehi and find out which way she has gone."

"You mean by divination? By magic?"

"Indian medicine . . . it works on the Apaches. Every time we take after them, the boys call on Desteen and he leads us right to the spot. Even when they send back scouts to watch for us, he locates them and the Navajos round them up. I'll ask the old man what he says."

He spoke to the medicine man, whose keen, dark eyes glowed as he pondered his reply.

"O-o!" he responded, and there was something in his bearing that roused a new hope in Lord Benedict. He was an old man, and yet not old, with firm white teeth that gleamed when he smiled on Silver Hat, and about his neck in heavy strands he wore a king's ransom in turquoise, the pay for many a long chant.

"He says he can do it," interpreted Silver Hat. "But, of course, you'll have to pay in advance. The medicine won't work unless you do. He passes the gift on to the gods."

"And to whom does he pray?" inquired his lordship.

"To Tinlehi, the green lizard they call Looks Like Ice, and to all the holy winds. He makes them offerings of corn pollen, and, if the gods are pleased, his hand comes down to the ground . . . so! That's a sign she is over there."

"Let us try it," suggested Lord Benedict eagerly, fetching out a golden sovereign, and Desteen pouched it gravely. Then he led the way to an empty house and prepared himself for the ceremony.

First he washed his hands and rolled up his right sleeve to the elbow, then, sitting on his heels and facing the east, he took out his sack of sacred corn pollen. Down the little finger of his right hand, while he prayed to Black Wind and Black Lizard, he strewed a line to his wrist, and so on down each finger, praying to the five holy winds and to Tinlehi, the lizard whose eyes look like ice. He ran a line down his forearm, around the inside of his thumb and out his middle finger to the tip, casting the remnant into the air. Then, touching pollen to his lips and to the top of his head, he threw it up into the heavens and bowed his head in earnest prayer.

"Holy Winds that blow from the five quarters of the earth, tell me the truth, where this woman is hidden. Holy Lizard, this man has made me a present. Now I offer this pollen to you. I want you to tell me everything. *Hozonlith* . . . it will be peaceful!"

As he prayed, his right arm was jerked up suddenly as if drawn by an unseen hand and he burst into a chant to the five holy winds and the far-seeing lizard—Tinlehi. His arm rose higher, lifting him up to his feet, and, palm upwards, he began to shake his hand sidewise.

"Where is the woman?" he asked in Navajo, and turned his shaking hand toward the east. But it did not strike down in assent. He began a solemn chant and turned his hand to the north, but still it shook sidewise in dissent. But when he moved it toward the west, it struck down, violently, and Desteen settled back, trembling.

"She is there," he said, pointing his finger to the northwest, and wiped the perspiration from his brow.

"But whereabouts?" demanded Lord Benedict incredulously.

"Over on Highest Mountain," answered Silver Hat. "He pointed in that direction. Just now we were going to the major to tell him of a vision that the old man had. He went off where it was quiet and looked at the sun and saw her alive through his crystal. She was riding on a horse and four Hopi snake priests were running along beside her."

"Incredible!" exclaimed Lord Benedict. "And yet why should we doubt it, when crystal gazing has been carried on for centuries? Would he consent to repeat his performance?"

"Not here," replied Silver Hat after a word with Desteen. "The medicine won't work when there are people around. Everything must be absolutely quiet. Even the horses and dogs have to be taken out of camp when the *hatali* looks at the stars. But when he gazed at the sun over the point of his crystal, its light became brighter and brighter, until suddenly he saw her, riding."

"And can he find her by this method of divining?"

"It's our last chance," responded Silver Hat. "The

only chance there is. The soldiers can never find her. But with a company of Navajo scouts and old Desteen, I believe I can locate her hiding place. I'll never give up trying as long as I know she's alive."

"Well said!" declared his lordship, laying a hand on his shoulder. "And I wish to thank you, my boy, for giving me something to hope for. She is my only child, the last of a noble line that has come down from William the Conqueror. No effort is too great, no price too high to pay, if only you can bring her back. May I offer a handful of sovereigns to give as fees to this grand old medicine man?"

He fetched out a fistful of his gold and thrust it forth so eagerly that Silver Hat took pity and accepted it.

"All right," he said, "the bigger the pay, the better the medicine works. But you've got to a place, Mister Benedict, where your money won't buy you anything."

"I know it, I know it," responded his lordship fervently. "I shall never forget your kindness. Now lead on to the major, and at another time I shall hope to be able to repay you."

Major Doyle was standing before the ruins of Masawa's house, making strange threats to the snake chief while Jani interpreted his remarks. But the fanatical old priest ignored him entirely—indeed, he seemed not to hear. His deep-set eyes were fixed, his lips moved soundlessly, and he smiled as if beholding some wondrous vision.

"He is talking to his son," whispered Desteen, regarding his rival with awe. "The Hopis have great magic power. They can talk without using words. We must be careful . . . do not speak before him."

"He says," interpreted Silver Hat, "that we'd better go away. Old Masawa is talking to his son."

"He is!" exclaimed Major Doyle. "Well, ask your old friend why *he* doesn't make some medicine."

"He has," returned Silver Hat, beckoning the major around the corner, "but he's afraid to talk before Masawa. So let's go into this house where no one will see us. He's located Lady Grace."

He spoke this last very low, after closing the door, and the major's gimlet eyes opened wide.

"How'd he find her?" he asked at last.

"By hand-shaking . . . and gazing at the sun. You know how the old man works."

"Well, where is she?" demanded the major impatiently.

"Over toward Highest Mountain, riding a horse along a trail. And four Hopi snake priests are with her."

"I believe it," declared Major Doyle. "Do you think you can find her if I send you with the scouts? We've played out our string with old Masawa . . . he'll never bring her back."

"We've got to find her," answered Silver Hat, "and be quick about it, too. But what about Harold Polinuivah? You heard what I said to his father."

"I heard you," returned the major, "but you'll receive no orders from me . . . except one. Bring back that woman . . . I don't care how. Bring her back if you have to kill every Hopi in the country. You're my last bet, Silver Hat. Good-bye."

He held out his hand and Silver Hat took it.

"I'll never come back till I find her," he said. "Watch for smoke." And he strode away.

CHAPTER TWELVE

A full twenty-four hours after she had been snatched from her father's side, the scouts took the trail to find Slender Woman. She had been spirited away as if by magic, and now the magic of the Navajos had been invoked to bring her back. Old Masawa had called upon the Hopi gods when his medicine was at the height of its power—when the snakes, holy messengers to Pahlulukangwi, were being borne away by the priests. Boldly and surely they grabbed them by the handful, scattering the soldiers right and left as they fled, and then, as Lady Grace stood stunned by the spectacle, she felt herself seized from behind. A white dancing blanket was thrown over her head and before she could even struggle she was thrust down into the storeroom.

Many hands laid hold of her, she was passed along from man to man, and with hardly a sound she felt herself descend down steps that could not be seen. Strong hands held her up, masterful hands that by their grip deprived her of the will to resist, and like one in a trance she submitted to the invisible forces that carried her down and down. Then a blast of cold air suddenly roused her from her apathy and she heard the tearing crash of lightning.

Snatching one hand free, she flung the blanket aside, but all about her was dark. There was rain in her face, and, as she struggled to escape, the lightning flashed again. Its angry, forked tongue seemed to strike directly at her as if the gods were intent on her destruction, and around her by its stark light she beheld grinning countenances—black faces, the huge mouths painted white. Then all became dark again as her head was covered and a strong man bore her on through the storm.

She felt the jar of his steps as he ran over rough ground, holding her firmly flung over his shoulder. The very elements turned against her, a furious rain beat upon them, and the man who carried her fell. But before she could escape, other arms caught her up and she was hurried, willy-nilly, on and on. Now she knew what was happening, for she had seen the painted snake priests. She was being carried away, despite the soldiers posted to guard her, but to what fate she could not imagine.

She remembered the stories of fair-haired women who had been taken from emigrant trains—women sought for far and wide yet never heard from again. Mrs. Adams and her two daughters given up for lost! Was she destined to follow in their steps? And what of Major Doyle and his sinister warnings? Had she perversely thrown away her own life? A thousand hopes and fears passed through her mind, leaving her dazed and dismayed by it all, and then, through the blanket, she heard Hopi voices, and her carrier came to a stop.

When she threw off the robe, she was surrounded by naked snake priests, their ceremonial feathers beaten flat by the rain, and Harold Polinuivah stood over her. She could see his painted face distorted in a smirk, for the moon had come through the clouds, but, although he ordered the priests about, he did not speak to her, and something bade her be still. She had fallen into the hands of cruel and desperate men and no pleadings could save her now. They had dared the wrath of Major Doyle himself—there was nothing to do but submit.

A horse was brought up and without a by-your-leave she was hoisted into the saddle. Then the flight was resumed, the men trotting ahead while her mount jogged along behind, and she broke his rough gait with the stirrups. Her white buckskin suit was soaked from the storm and the midnight wind was cold, but she wrapped herself in the dancing blanket and endured without a word. Now that the first shock was past, her courage had returned and she looked about for some means of escape. But the runners who fled before her, as tireless as automatons, now carried short lances in their hands. They had war clubs in their belts, bows and arrows in short quivers, and round rawhide shields on their arms. The Peace People had turned warriors, and, as they ran, they looked back at their prize.

A dark cañon loomed before them and they plunged into the Stygian shadows, never breaking their pace for the boulders that blocked the way, dragging her pony relentlessly on. Then they came out into the moonlight, and, as the night wore away, they entered a forest of cedars. Dawn found them on the brink of a deep cañon and for the first time Harold spoke.

"Get down," he said. "This is very steep trail. But do not try to run away. Many snake priests come behind."

She clambered down stiffly and sank to the ground while Polinuivah smiled.

"You tired," he said. "What you think of Hopis now? My people run all night."

"You are bad people, Harold," she answered sternly. "Major Doyle will punish you for this."

"No. Not punish," he said. "Soldiers never come here. This is home of my ancestors, many hundred years ago, and nobody comes but us."

"I saw Silver Hat there," she suggested. "He and his scouts will follow your tracks."

"Cannot follow tracks," he leered. "Big rain wash them out. You think Silver Hat is smart? He can never find you now. If he follows, this will kill him." He plucked a short arrow from his quiver and pointed to the tip. "Poison," he said. "Only snake priests can make it. Not quick poison . . . very slow . . . body rot away. Maybe six months, but sure to die."

"Oh, be careful!" she cried as he flipped the arrow about, but Harold only laughed.

"My people have medicine to cure," he said. "This poison is for Navajos, if they come. You see men by rock? That is guard . . . to watch trail. So now you can never go back."

He looked at her strangely and Lady Grace summoned all her courage.

"What do you intend to do with me, Harold?" she asked. "Haven't I always been your friend?"

"Yes," he answered, but without his old smile. "You are good friend of all the Peace People. We are sorry we have to steal you. All the Hopitu like you . . . they think you are god. Come from Sun's home, other side of Eastern Ocean."

"Oh, really!" she cried, although her heart sank a little. "Is that why they took me, Harold?"

"Long time ago," he expounded soberly, "Hopi prophet said you would come."

"And for what purpose?" she asked at last.

"I will tell you by and by," he responded evasively. "But now all my people are your friends. Here is bread for you to eat . . . *peekee* bread my mother made. And here is a piece of meat."

He produced some thin, blue wafers and a meager strip of dried meat, laying them down in their wrappings before her, then he sat back benignly and watched her eat while the Hopis consumed their own food.

"I am warrior now," he said, "and new warriors do not eat. All the men of the snake clan are warriors. We are men with the hands and the feet. We are not afraid of anything."

"Why, I thought," she exclaimed, "that the Hopis were Peace People!"

"Yes . . . Peace People." He nodded. "But not all. Hopis have war clans, too . . . brave men who go first to battle. We have medicine to make our hearts strong."

"Then why," she asked, "does your father thrust out his neck and tell the soldiers to kill him? I thought you were all non-resistants."

"Only common people," he said. "And soldiers will not kill him. Our prophets knew everything, and long time ago they told us the White People would come. You are the children of that oldest brother who never had done anything wrong. The Yucca Man told him to go to the east till he came to the land of the Sun. Then to bow down and touch his head to the Sun and come back to Kahwestimah, his old home. After that certain things would happen . . . I will tell you by and by."

He lapsed into a calm, smiling silence, and Lady Grace glanced about. All the others had retired up the trail to where two rocks made a narrow defile. It was a natural gateway, protecting the cañon below, whose depth she could barely sense. That it was wide she knew from the large cliff of red sandstone that appeared across a break in the trees, but what was down below she could only guess—some hiding place, where she would never be found. She drew a deep breath and asked the fatal question, and once more Polinuivah smiled.

"Big cliff dwellings," he answered, "built by Snake People, long ago. You like to go down and see? Holy place for the snake clan. Long time ago one Spanish man come here and write his name in the mud. You like to see his name? Dated sixteen sixty-one."

"Why, how interesting!" she exclaimed. "Yes, I would . . . some other time. But, Harold, this has gone far enough. I want you to take me back!"

He gazed at her curiously, as if he had not understood.

"Back to soldiers?" he asked at last.

"Yes, back to my father," she responded firmly. "If you do, he will pay you well."

"No. You come with me," he coaxed.

"But I tell you," she cried, "I don't want to go!"

"You come," he said again.

"No!" she stormed.

Harold Polinuivah smiled. "Yes," he said. "You come."

CHAPTER THIRTEEN

Lady Grace caught her breath and looked at Harold again, and suddenly her heart seemed to stop. A hundred generations of soldiers were behind her, the best fighting blood of old England, but a great fear clutched at her throat. She was trapped, and the bold stare of Polinuivah's eyes made her think of slimy monsters, twining snakes. His education had fallen away like a cloak and he stood forth a naked savage.

"You come," he said again, and at the touch of his hand she leaped up and faced him, panting. But as she opened her mouth to speak, her courage failed—she had found her master at last.

"Down in cañon," he went on, "many Hopi ladies comes. Pretty soon we have big dance . . . sing songs to Mother Earth. You like to see old ceremony? You like to dance with ladies? All right, I take you down."

He led down the trail, and, after a last glance behind, Lady Grace followed him reluctantly. Like a

lost soul entering the stark labyrinths of Hades,
forced on against her will yet lacking the courage to
turn back, she picked her way down narrow chasms
and rocky slopes until suddenly she beheld the
abyss. It descended terrace by terrace to a last final
dip, and over its brink appeared the tops of cottonwood trees following a tiny thread of water.

"Snake Cañon," announced Harold. "My people
call it Chua. Home of snake clan, long time ago."

"But how do you get down?" she quavered.

"Nice path," he said. "You come." Once more she
lacked the power to resist. There was something in
the gleam of his smiling brown eyes that swayed her
against her will. In his hands she was helpless, ruled
over by a fear that killed all lesser fears. The trail
swung in zigzags along the face of the slanting cliff,
descending from terrace to terrace by steps cut into
the rock and she followed without a word. Her
knees trembled, her body quaked, and she felt her
senses reel, but she dared not refuse to obey. On the
edge of the last chasm she halted and drew back, too
terrified to take another step. Down the face of the
steep slope a row of footholds led, each hole a mere
cat step for the sure feet of cliff dwellers, but full of
dangers for her.

"You come," beckoned Harold, and blindly she
made the attempt. Step by step she slid down,
clutching the sandstone with both hands, while
Polinuivah walked upright before her, and, as he
looked back, she caught the glint of malevolent
laughter in those eyes she had once deemed so fine.
But now the devil came out in him and he gloated
over her weakness.

"All right," he said as she reached the bottom and

fell down in the sand, "you think the soldiers come here? You think your friend Silver Hat chase Hopis to this place? Snake warriors will kill him, sure."

Lady Grace rose slowly, ignoring his boasts, and crept to the stream for a drink. Then she bathed her wind-burned face while he watched her curiously, like a cat that plays with a mouse. But as he gazed, his hard eyes changed and he spoke to her more gently.

"All my people," he said, "they think you are a god. But me, I think you are a woman. Very pretty woman, too . . . you like to marry me? My father is chief of Kahwestimah."

"No, Harold," she answered without looking up, and the hard look came back into his eyes.

"Come on," he ordered, and in sullen silence he led the way down the cañon.

High sandstone cliffs rose on either side, their sheer walls stained by long streaks of black where the water had seeped from the rim, and far above, light as air, the blue martins dipped and played, oblivious of human misery. Then they rounded a point and, under the brow of a shattered cliff, Lady Grace beheld the cliff dwellings. Square houses of stone and mud clung along the narrow shelf like the nests of the swallows above them, and, leading down to the bottom, there came a line of foot holes like the tracks of a bug in sand.

Generations before, with no tools but harder stones, the ancient cliff dwellers, the ancestors of the Snake People, had pecked that line of tracks. Then patiently, rock by rock, they had borne up the square-edged stones and lain them in walls along the shelf. Lady Grace gazed in awe at this, her first cliff dwelling, forgetting her weariness in the presence of this monument to the fears of vanished centuries. But as she paused, an old woman stepped out of a doorway—the dwellings were peopled once more.

"There's a woman!" she exclaimed, and Harold turned back, smiling.

"My aunt," he said. "You like to stay with her? All right . . . we climb up there."

He led the way up the winding steps, worn deep by many feet, and, as Lady Grace mounted to the shelf of rock, the old hag bowed and muttered.

"She says you are her daughter," interpreted Polinuivah. "She will show you place to sleep."

"Ah, ah!" responded the woman, beckoning eagerly, and Lady Grace passed through the door. Whatever her fate she could think of nothing now but to drop down and go to sleep—anything to forget the weariness that made her an unthinking clod. A rabbit-skin robe was spread out on the floor and with a sigh she sank down and slept.

When she awoke, it was dark, and the air was pulsating to the steady beat of a drum. A chorus of deep voices took up a measured chant as she lay listening, afraid to move, and her heart gave a great leap and stopped. The snake priests were there—they had come while she slept. Was she to be offered up as a sacrifice? The dark hints of Polinuivah, his frank proposal of marriage, took another and more sinister color. Was he trying to save her from a fate still worse, such as had blotted out the lives of the rest? What manner of men were these Snake People? She rose softly and crept to the door.

From the mouth of a kiva built back against the wall there came the glow of a hidden fire. The moon, bright as day, lit up the valley below, but, as she stepped out, a dark form sprang up. Lying against the wall of the house like a dog on guard a ragged-headed Hopi greeted her coming with a grunt and the point of a naked lance. She gasped and leaped back, too startled to make an outcry. Was this the treatment due a goddess?

With sinking heart she crept back to her bed, spread out on the bare dirt floor, but as the hours dragged by, sleep claimed her again, and, when she awoke, it was day. The old woman had come in to lay a fire in the corner and Lady Grace summoned up a smile. Then she stepped to the door and Harold Chasing Butterflies looked up from his place against the wall. If she could only win him over and escape!

"May I come out?" she asked, and Harold gave an answering smile.

"Yes. Come out," he said. "How you feel?"

"Quite rested," she replied, keeping her distance. "But what was the singing last night?"

"Practice song for big dance tonight. Now every-body gone away."

"It is all very strange," she murmured. "May I walk around, Harold, and look?"

"Pretty soon," he said, "I show you everything. You have breakfast . . . then we talk."

Lady Grace retired to her prison cell and broke her fast meagerly on parched corn paste thinned with water. The room seemed quite bare of any other food and the old woman grumbled as she ate.

"She says,"—Harold grinned—"that corn is 'most gone. Then what will she have to eat?"

"Yes? What will she have?" inquired Grace.

"More people come today," he said. "Maybeso they bring some corn. Lots of ladies come over, to Mother Earth Dance. Very beautiful . . . never been seen before."

"You mean"—she smiled—"that I am to see it? I remember you invited me, long ago."

"If you want to," he answered, going on with his eating. "But maybe you like to stay here."

He gave her a quick glance and laughed to himself, but Lady Grace made no reply. There was something about him that made her fear Harold, no matter how kindly he smiled, and when, after breakfast, they went out in the sun, she felt that her hour had come. Whatever her fate she would know it soon, for a strange light had come into his eyes.

"You like sun?" he inquired ingratiatingly. "You like to sit here and get warm? Hopi people same way . . . we think sun is everything. Say prayers and sing songs to Father Sun."

"Yes?" she responded as he smiled complacently, and Harold went glibly on.

"Long time ago Father Sun and Mother Earth, they love each other very much. Sun shine on earth and earth have many flowers. Like children, you understand. All flowers, all butterflies, all beautiful things. Now every year when corn is getting ripe, Hopi people have dance to Sun. Pray to Mother Earth, too, to send lots of everything . . . lots of corn, lots of beans, lots of melons. Maybeso tonight you go to see dance. Come on, I show you around."

He jumped up nimbly and led the way along the terrace where small, half-closed doors opened into musty rooms as dark as a coyote's den. Then he climbed up slowly toward a mud-plastered wall on which a name and date had been written.

"You see?" he said, tracing the date with his finger. "Was made in sixteen sixty-one."

"Why, yes!" she exclaimed. "This is where some Spaniard wrote long ago. Did he live with your people, Harold?"

"Yes . . . live here," he answered gravely. "Took best house, you see, and plastered all over again. Then write his name in mud. He was priest, you understand."

"And what happened to him?" asked Lady Grace curiously.

"I don't know . . . maybe die," suggested Harold lightly. "Hopi people have own religion. Now I tell you what you asked me yesterday, about Yucca Man and Oldest Brother. Long time ago we have prophet named Mahcheedo . . . he is man that said you would come. Beautiful woman with yellow hair would come from beyond the ocean and her son would become great chief, to lead Hopis against all their enemies."

" 'Her son,' " she repeated aghast, and then she went quickly on. "But how could they conquer their enemies? The Hopis are not warriors."

"How you think," he demanded, "we kill Utes and Navajos? The Snakes are warrior clan. You see that pouch we wear in Snake Dance? Full of scalps or bones of enemy. Your people are warriors, too?"

"Oh, yes," she responded, "my father is a colonel in the British army. When we came to America, the English chief gave us letters, requesting the great chief in Washington to tell all his soldiers to protect us. That is why Major Doyle took so many men to guard us when we came to see the Snake Dance. If you do not send me back, Harold, all your people will be killed."

"Oh, no." He laughed. "That is what other women said, but none of my people killed. You see me come to fort? You see me talk to major? Nothing happened, only soldiers were mad. They ride around everywhere, but cannot find white women."

"Where are they?" she asked, after a pause.

"You like to see them?" he asked, but Lady Grace could not answer. A great fear was clutching at her throat.

"You come," he said, laying a hand on her arm, "I show you something else."

He led the way to the topmost tier of houses, far back in the chill depths of the cavern, and she followed like one in a dream.

"Long time ago," he said, "when Snake People build this place, we have different kind of girl, very white, called They Upon Whom The Sun Never Shines. They live in these houses with door only in top, so face will never tan. Make girls very pretty, and, before they are married, young men come and talk down hole. Hopis call them engagement rooms. You like to look in here?"

He pointed to an opening, walled up breast high, in the roof of the topmost room, but she shook her head and drew back.

"Yes, you look." he urged, and, fascinated, she leaned over and gazed down into the gloom.

All was dark, but from the depths a faint moan reached her ears, and, as she strained her eyes, three frail forms appeared, lying prostrate on the floor.

"What is it?" she demanded, her eyes big with horror, and his pouting lips parted in a smile.

"Other white women," he said. "But no good! Not the ones that Mahcheedo prophesied. They would not go to Mother Earth Dance. So now we are letting them die."

"Why, Harold," she cried, starting back, "how can you be so cruel?"

"That is Snake religion," he responded imperturbably. "You like to go down there, too?"

"Oh, no." She shuddered. "No! No!"

"Then must go to dance with me."

"'Must?'" she repeated, looking up, and Harold nodded.

"Very beautiful ceremony," he said. "To Mother Earth and Father Sun. Hopi ladies all come, one for every priest, and you can dance with me."

"No!" she gasped, and his hard eyes turned to agate.

"Yes!" he answered, and waited, his hand on the engagement room wall.

She turned her face away and stood trembling. Then at last she raised her head.

"I will go," she said. "But if you touch me, I will kill you."

"Oh, no," he protested. "No touch. Ladies stand in one line, men stand in other, and dance back and forth by fire. That is better than staying down there."

He glanced into the depths of the black cell before them and Lady Grace nodded, weeping. Anything was better than that.

CHAPTER FOURTEEN

Trembling in every limb, her heart frozen with fear, Lady Grace left the chill of the charnel house behind her and crept down into the sun. The world had gone black like that dark and fetid hole that held three fair-haired women like she. But as she sat on the terrace of the cliff dwellings and gazed up at the swallows at play, a thought came to her suddenly that the soldiers were near, and all her old courage returned. She had seen in a swift vision Silver Hat, riding hard, followed by Jani and old Desteen and a squad of Navajo scouts.

Other thoughts sprang up, crowding out of her harried mind the memory of what seemed only a dream, but at dawn they had really come to the forest of cedars—even at this moment they were riding its dim trails. In and out among the trees, urging their horses to a lope, the Navajos whipped along in the wake of Silver Hat's hat until at last he came to a halt.

"My grandfather," he said, "try your hand-shaking

once more. There is no end to this forest, but the winds blow everywhere and Tinlehi has eyes that see far. Perhaps we have gone the wrong way."

He took from his pocket one of the English sovereigns that Lord Benedict had thrust upon him, yet, although Desteen prayed and sang, the medicine would not work—his hand hung, dead and limp.

"We have come the wrong way!" clamored the Navajos in chorus. "Why look for Hopis in this wilderness where not even coyotes live?"

"Nevertheless," responded Silver Hat, "we will try again. Hold your horses by the head and do not let them snort while my father and I pray to the sun."

He dismounted wearily after his long night in the saddle, and with Desteen in the lead they walked far to the east, where no noise could break in on their trance. Then from the sack that held his corn pollen Desteen took out a rock crystal, five-pointed like a fallen star, and bowed his head in prayer. Into his eyes he rubbed pollen that had been wet with the eye water of an eagle and the dust of clear crystals to aid his sight. Then he sang to the gods and, holding the crystal between two fingers, pointed the tip of it straight into the sun.

"I see Slender Woman," he said at last. "She is sitting in front of a cliff dwelling, and Jedih, the Antelope, is with her."

"Your medicine is good," responded Silver Hat. "But where are there cliff dwellings around here?"

"*Hola* . . . I don't know," sighed Desteen. "My hand said they took her to the north."

"We will go north, then," answered Silver Hat. And once more at the head of his men he went loping through the cedars. But the sun rose high, their horses slacked their pace, and before them there was nothing but trees.

"There are no cañons here," grumbled the Navajos, and at last Silver Hat pulled up short. Over the tips of the giant cedars Highest Mountain rose before them, an eagle glided by, but the cañon of the cliff dwellings had not been found and the time was passing fast.

"We are lost," said Silver Hat, and, reaching into his pocket, he fetched out a handful of sovereigns. "My grandfather," he went on, "here is an offering to Tinlehi and the winds that see everything as they pass. Every piece of gold is worth five dollars in silver. Ask the gods where Slender Woman is."

Desteen took the money and went off to the east, with only Silver Hat to watch, and, after praying long and earnestly, he shook pollen on his hand and sang to Tinlehi, the lizard.

> Black Lizard. At his hogan he rubs a rock on my
>   hand.
> Black Lizard. At his hogan he rubs a rock on my
>   hand.
> Yellow Lizard. At his hogan he rubs a rock on my
>   hand.
> White Lizard. At his hogan he rubs a rock on my
>   hand.
> Spotted Lizard. At his hogan he rubs a rock on
>   my hand.

His hand rose up higher; it trembled to and fro. Then suddenly it was jerked into the air, shaking violently from side to side.

"Is she there?" demanded Desteen, pointing his hand to the east. But the shaking hand answered: No.

"Is she there?" he asked again. And, when he turned to the north, the hand struck down to the earth.

"She is before us," the old man announced, and once more the scouts loped north. Highest Mountain loomed higher, the ground became broken, and then across their way a great cañon appeared and they halted on the brink of a precipice.

"Ho!" exclaimed the warriors after a long, impressive silence, and Silver Hat searched the cliffs with his field glasses.

"This is the place," he said at last. "I can see far ahead the little houses the enemy ancestors built. My grandfather's medicine is good."

Then they whipped ahead, riding parallel to the cañon that cut the high country in twain, and opposite the ruins Silver Hat crept out again to look down into the abyss. From the fringe of cedars that overhung its brink, the red sandstone wall went straight down, but on the opposite side, where the cliff had been shattered, a great section had fallen away. There in silent rows stood the ancient dwellings of the Anasuzzi, the enemy ancestors of the Hopis. But the cañon was void of life. In jagged twists and turns it lost itself in nothingness, and Silver Hat lowered his glasses with a sigh. But Jani, crouching beside him, clutched his master by the arm and pointed back at the ruins.

"Hopi," he muttered, and, when Silver Hat looked again, he saw a man, climbing up the stone steps. In all that vast valley he was the only speck of life but he proved that their medicine was good. He was a

Hopi, stripped to a G-string, his hair banged in front, and Silver Hat followed him curiously through his field glasses. Like an ape, with long, skinny arms that felt ahead as he climbed, he mounted the deeply worn trail, and, as he hurried along the shelf, his sharp, wizened profile came suddenly into view. It was Masawa, the snake chief, and yet only the day before they had left him a prisoner at Red Mesa.

Silver Hat muttered to himself as he spied his archenemy, but the next moment he spat out a curse. From the black doorway of a house Polinuivah had stepped forth, still attired in the kilt of a snake priest. They met and turned back, and at the entrance to the house the old man bent over and peered in.

"There she is," breathed Silver Hat, but they moved away, and he watched for Lady Grace in vain. "She is in there," he insisted to Jani. "Shut up in that room. But where is the trail that leads down?"

Jani pointed in silence up the cañon, which had suddenly come to life. Around the point a long procession had appeared and Silver Hat passed the glasses to his friend.

"Hopi women," pronounced Jani. "They have come for a dance. See, their legs are painted white."

"What dance?" demanded Silver Hat.

"Don't know"—Jani shrugged, still looking—"maybeso old dance they have. When Hopis have this dance, nobody can come into village for three days. Long time ago Spanish missionaries tried to pass, but Monkey People killed them all."

"What kind of a dance?" repeated Silver Hat anxiously, and Jani groped for words.

"Some people call it Adam and Eve Dance," he said at last. "They sing to Mother Earth, to make everything grow. Lots of corn, lots of lambs . . . lots of babies, too. All the strong young men and women go. They drink a kind of love medicine. I think that is what it is."

"My . . . God!" exclaimed Silver Hat, drawing back. "Is that why they've come out here?"

"I think so," responded Jani mildly. "There are snake priests, coming up."

Silver Hat snatched at his glasses and looked down the valley, where a procession of men had appeared. They were stripped to the waist, their bodies painted red, and each wore a huge, disk-shaped mask. They marched lustily, singing a song that came up to him faintly like the roar of breakers on the shore, but, as they passed the cliff dwelling, old Masawa bounded forth and halted them with outstretched hand. They waited, watching the path, and at last from a doorway Polinuivah appeared with Lady Grace. For a moment she hesitated, then came slowly down and joined them, and the deep chant rose again.

"Hurry up, now," advised Jani as Silver Hat lay staring. "When moon rises, dance begins."

CHAPTER FIFTEEN

Once more the jaded horses were lashed to a gallop as Silver Hat led his scouts north, but at a turn of the cañon their dash was cut short—a deep chasm appeared before them. They swung east, to pass around it, but, as they neared its head, Desteen held up his hand. Then, touching his lips for silence, he sang his song to the winds, for something told him that enemies were near. He raised his arm toward the east and his hand struck down.

"Hopis," he said, and took the lead on foot, while the others dismounted and followed. He crept around a point and beckoned to Silver Hat, and at a gash between two rocks where a trail passed through stood two Hopis, masked. They were stripped to the waist, their bodies were painted red, and from the center of their round masks red points shot out to represent the rays of the sun. Each bore a bow and arrow and a short, red lance, but they were looking the other way.

"What is your word?" inquired Desteen, creeping

close to Silver Hat. "Whoa Besh"—by which he meant Major Doyle—"has told the Navajos we must kill no more Hopis, but these are guarding the trail."

"He gave me only one order," answered Silver Hat. "To bring Slender Woman back. And since these men stand in our way . . ."

"Good." Desteen nodded, and, unwrapping his war bundle, he brought out a Hopi scalp. Then, hiding behind a rock, he made war medicine over it while the Navajos painted their faces.

"The war god," he announced, coming back stripped for battle, "has made the Hopi men foolish. He has made their eyes blind. Their ears are stopped up. There is no strength in their arms and legs."

"Good," responded Silver Hat. "Now who will creep up on them and shoot them both dead with arrows?"

"The Hopis killed my mother," spoke up Jani, stepping forth. "My arrow will not fail."

"I will go with you, my brother," said another young warrior, and Silver Hat motioned them on.

They glided forward swiftly, for the sun was hanging low and the trail down the cañon was long, and, as he watched them through his glasses, Silver Hat saw a Hopi pitch forward with an arrow sticking out of his back. The other had turned to flee when another arrow struck him down, and the two Navajos leaped upon them. Then the scouts went galloping in to where the two bodies lay stripped, and Silver Hat snatched up a mask.

"My grandfather," he said to Desteen, "paint my body like these dead Hopis while I put on their clothes and this mask. I am going down the trail alone, to bring back Slender Woman."

"It is good," replied Desteen, "for if they see the Navajos coming, they will kill her with poisoned arrows."

Then he went to work swiftly, saying nothing, and the scouts gathered around to help.

"What shall we do when you are gone?" one asked, and Silver Hat eyed him sternly.

"Stay here, my brothers," he said, "and kill every Hopi that comes. I am going on a dangerous mission and the way must be kept open behind. But if I do not return by dawn, follow after me and take revenge."

"We will kill them, every one," promised Jani. "I am your slave. I have given you my warrior's name. I swear to avenge your death."

"You are my brother," corrected Silver Hat, taking his hand. "Wear my hat and ride my horse, until I come back. And if I die, all I have is yours." Turning to Desteen, he said: "My grandfather, I will never come back until I find Slender Woman and take her away from the Hopis. I do not know where I will go. So pray to Tinlehi and look through your crystal, and follow to wherever I am. For if I come too late to save her from Polinuivah, I will bury this in his heart."

He touched the knife that he had hidden in his belt and darted off down the trail, and, just as night was falling, he set foot in the cañon below. In the world above the full moon was slowly rising, painting the west wall of the chasm with a silvery light that accentuated the ghostly darkness of the pit. But as he groped his way forward, the silence was broken by the sound of a distant drum.

It beat slowly, insistently, as if summoning priests and maidens, wherever they were, to come, and, as

Silver Hat hurried toward it, he had a vision of Lady Grace, led captive to her fate. Through the eye-holes of his mask he could see against the sky the ruddy glow of a fire, but it was hidden from sight by the cleft walls of a side cañon that encircled the dance ground within. From the outer darkness he could catch the gleam of flames and the blink as dancers went past, but the bed of the cañon was obstructed with trees and at the entrance two armed warriors stood guard.

Silver Hat crept closer, disguised by his mask, ready to pass in if others took the lead, but, as he crouched back, watching, white forms appeared before him. It was the procession of women, walking softly through the darkness, their bodies shrouded in ceremonial blankets, their legs wrapped in white buskins to the knees. They passed in decorously, their heads bent low, their black hair over their faces for a mask, but there was one head near the end that was not black. It was fair—the golden head of Lady Grace!

Silver Hat started up, trembling, ready to fight his way in and snatch her away from her guards, but before he could act, another procession stepped out into the feeble light of the fire. They had come from up the cañon, the stalwart warriors of the snake clan, their naked bodies painted red with white lightning striking down—and each man bore a lance. One by one, in kilts and moccasins, they passed by the silent guards, laying their spears down in a pile as they disappeared into the willows. Silver Hat circled about, joining the end of the line, and passed safely through with the rest.

Along the bank of a tiny creek the masked procession moved and, willy-nilly, he went with it. Beneath the overhanging trees, trodden smooth by many feet, the path wound in and out, until suddenly, as they rounded a point through a grove of ancient cottonwoods, the dancing ground came into view. It was a smooth, grassy *redondo*, picked clean of sticks and stones—a round, level spot, flanked on both sides by willows, which turned into a thicket above. The snake priests led off arrogantly, but, as they advanced into the firelight, Silver Hat dodged back and plunged under a tree. The next minute the two guards came noiselessly down the trail and stopped a scant spear's length away.

From the depths of the black shadow that covered him like a shroud, Silver Hat could see nothing but their towering masks and the gleam of their painted arms. He lay still, and, as he waited, the drumming suddenly ceased and a low, solemn chant rose up. There was a long, aching silence while the fire burned low and the moonlight, inch by inch, crept down the western wall until at last it touched the field. Then peering through the branches, Silver Hat saw old Masawa stooping over a huge earthen bowl.

At its base the glowing coals of the dying fire supplied heat for his magic brew, and as, potion by potion, he cast in the ingredients, he muttered prayers to his pagan gods. Stepping out into the bright moonlight, he raised his hands to the sky, throwing up corn pollen to the gods, then, stooping to the ground, he prayed to Mother Earth and the drummer smote his drum. From the darkness, dim forms came hurrying to the fire, which now hurled up showers of sparks, and, as the flames leaped up, the two guardsmen moved closer while a wild, rhyth-

mic chant began. Like a long, spidery ape old Masawa leaped to and fro, adding herbs to his witch
pot, dipping out a gourd full to taste, until at last his
love medicine was done.

Silver Hat caught a great breath as, from the
shadow of the cottonwoods, the procession of
women marched forth. While they waited beneath
the trees, they had woven chaplets of broad leaves to
hold back their flowing hair, and now, masked behind it, they advanced one by one to drink from the
passion-rousing bowl. Masawa stood beside it, dipping a gourd for each, and, as they drained it to the
dregs, he sprinkled them with corn pollen, throwing the last pinch into the air for the gods.

Smoothly painted with white clay, their swelling
bosoms were now bare, for their blankets had been
cast aside, and in the light of the roaring fire they
appeared warmly voluptuous where before they
had been shame-faced and shy. They drank eagerly
and deeply while, from the darkness beyond, the
bass chorus of the men rose and fell. But when Lady
Grace appeared, upheld by a huge Amazon, the
thunder of their voices ceased. She, too, was clad
only in buskins and skirt and the golden tresses of
her hair, but about her there lingered a beauty such
as no savage woman could possess.

She stood there, trembling before the bowl, looking wildly about, struggling feebly against her fate,
then resignedly she quaffed the drink and, chatter-
ing avidly, old Masawa cast pollen on her breast. In
the shadows Silver Hat clutched at his knife, every
nerve afire to strike. But before him, lance in hands,
the two warriors stood their guard, and he crouched
back, biding his time. They were deep in the narrow

cañon, surrounded by savage foes, and to move now might mean death to both Silver Hat and Slender Woman.

A deadly apathy came over him as, man after man, the snake priests marched up and drank. In the ruddy gleam of the fire their bodies seemed made of bronze, as tough and enduring as steel. They would strike him down as ruthlessly as killing a spider if he broke in on this orgy of love. There was a fire in their eyes that told of smoldering passions that soon would be fanned to hot flame. Yet dare their anger he must or Lady Grace would meet a fate worse than death.

Now the long line was ended and the masked satyrs went bounding back, and in two lines facing each other the men and women stood apart, swaying slowly, hand in hand. The rousing drum boomed out, a wild chant began, and with rhythmic steps they raised their hands to Father Sun and reached down to salute Mother Earth. They danced nearer and floated back like butterflies at play, the white forms of the women like sprites in the firelight, the men like living bronze. The mad fire of the love medicine was coursing through their veins; they stepped faster, with amorous stamps, but always, as they met, the line of women gave back while the warriors came on and on.

They raised their faces to the sky where the moon in all her splendor shone down upon their bacchanal, then, bowing low, they almost touched the earth, the source of life and love. But always the men came on and on and the women gave way before them. Then suddenly, with a yell that made Silver

Hat's heart stand still, the lines broke—and the women were gone. The dark shadows of the trees gave back a twinkle of fleeing forms, and like hawks, each marking down his prey, the masked warriors plunged in after them.

CHAPTER SIXTEEN

Last of all in the rout of dancing women, fleeing blindly because they fled, Lady Grace darted wildly into the black corridors of the thicket while Silver Hat stared after her, dazed. But when a lithe warrior dashed eagerly after her, he broke cover like a charging elk. Knocking the armed guards aside, he plunged across the dancing ground, smashing his mask against the limbs as he dove into the tunnel that wild animals had made through the willows.

Brush crashing to the right and left, he caught flashing glimpses of women with men in close pursuit, then from the passageway before him there came a frightened scream—Lady Grace's voice crying for help. His hair bristled with fury and a mad despair as he fought his way through the trees, and, as he broke into the open, he heard a man's voice, laughing—the voice of Harold Polinuivah.

It had been a long chase, this pursuit of Slender Woman, but at last she was in his power. He held her tightly as with frightened intensity she struggled to tear herself free, and, as they swayed back and forth, he chuckled exultantly, giving her time to wear herself down. But suddenly a strong hand laid hold of his shoulder and he was hurled back into the brush.

In the darkness the white form of Lady Grace stood wraith-like as she shrank before the new invader, then, cursing in Hopi, Polinuivah charged and Silver Hat struck with all his might. But no blow from the dark could turn back Harold. He grunted and came on and, with the strength of ten men, Silver Hat crushed the Indian in his arms. Then, swiftly changing hands, he whipped out his hidden knife and stabbed him to the heart. There was a gush of hot blood, the tense body relaxed, but when Silver Hat hurled him aside and turned to Grace, she had disappeared into the night.

With desperate haste he groped his way along the trail, looking to right and left as he passed, and just as his heart went dead from fear he found her, prone in the path. She had fainted as she fled and he caught her up quickly, still burning with white-hot anger at the Hopi who had dared to bring her to this. But now he lay still in a pool of his own blood and there was barely time to escape.

Pressing his way through the willows, Silver Hat circled to the north, and, as he peered into the open, he could see old Masawa, beating the drum with all his might. His gray hair was flying, his low-browed head thrown back, and, as he beat, he bawled forth a wild chant. But the dancing ground was empty; even the guards had disappeared. Crouching low, Silver Hat bore Grace away. To him, she was Lady Grace no longer—only a woman, lying helplessly in his arms.

Down the dark trail, through patches of moonlight that lighted up her pale face, he ran until at last he came to the mouth of the cañon and sank down in the grass. The last of his strength was spent, his breath came in choking gasps, but she lay so still that he leaned over her anxiously, brushing back the tangled hair from her eyes.

The chaplet of torn leaves, the golden locks, the drooping head, reminded him vaguely of a Christ picture he had seen—but she had not been crucified. She had escaped the profanation the ruthless Peace People had planned for her, and now, breathing softly, she lay in his arms like a child that had fallen asleep. He gathered her up gently and staggered on down the cañon, but at his touch she opened her eyes.

"Dear Silver Hat," she said, smiling up at him. "I knew you would come and save me. But put me down here . . . and lean closer. There is something I wish to say."

He lay her down, startled at the strange look in her eyes. They were wide open and dilated, and, as he held his head closer, she twined her slender arms about his neck.

"I love you," she breathed. "I love no one but you. Ever since that day when you saved me from the Hopis . . . will you give me another kiss?"

He jerked his head away and stared down at her curiously. There was a look on her face he had never seen before—a sweet, adoring smile that put him under a breathless spell. And it seemed unreal.

"No," he said, drawing back. "This is no place for kissing. I have killed Polinuivah. The Hopis will soon be after us. Get up, and see if you can walk."

"No, no," she coaxed. "I am tired now. And

something is hurting my head. Just hold me in your arms and let me rest a while. Don't you love me, my Galahad?"

He gazed at her again and in a flash it came over him—she was drugged, under the influence of the love medicine that old Masawa had brewed for the dancers. This was no love for him, but the effect of a philter—her eyes were dark with passion.

"No!" he cried, snatching her up and starting down the cañon, but, as he held her closely, she drew down his head and kissed him again and again. Sudden fire ran through his veins as her hot lips met his—he stumbled and sank to the ground. Then, patiently, he released the arms that clung to him and put her away with a sigh. A madness had come over him, a reckless longing to forget everything and submit to each loving caress, but the kisses were not for him. He lay her down gently in the warm, soft sand and turned his face away.

"Silver Hat, dear," she breathed, "there is something I wish to tell you. I never knew love till you took me in your arms and carried me up to your cabin. But the Benedicts are proud of their noble blood . . . we are taught never to love a commoner. And I had plighted my troth to Lionel. That is why, when you kissed me, I slapped you in the face. Can you forgive me? Can you understand?"

"Don't talk," he warned. "The Hopis might hear you."

"But I must talk," she pleaded. "I must tell you the rest. I am never going back to Lionel. It was to escape marrying him that I came to this country . . . and now I have found you, dear Silver Hat."

She drew him down impulsively and pressed her

lips to his, and once more he felt his senses reel.
Worn and weary as he was, he knew the sudden ecstasy of a woman's passionate embrace. There was
nothing in the world but this soft, clinging creature
whose body lay so close to his—nothing to think of,
nothing to resist. And yet he must resist! Into his
ears, as he knelt beside her, there came a loud, startled yell and the clamor of angry shouts.

"They are coming," he whispered, catching her
up from the ground, and with the last of his
strength he ran on until he stepped into a hole and
fell. Then he lay there, breathing heavily, while out
in the moonlight a party of Hopis dashed past. They
returned, still running, and, as the hue and cry went
on, Silver Hat roused up and looked around. He
had fallen over the edge of a low cutbank and into
its blackest shade, but the floor of the great cañon
was white beneath the moon and he could see that
his retreat was cut off. Up the long zigzag trail that
led to the rim a line of vengeful Hopis were swarming like ants.

"Come on," he muttered, turning to Lady Grace,
who lay motionlessly where she had fallen, and,
when he touched her, she did not respond. She had
fainted, and from a pool he dipped up a handful of
water and dashed it into her face.

"Oh!" she cried, starting up. "Where am I? What
is it?"

"Keep still," he hissed. "It's Silver Hat."

He dragged her down, behind the rampart of the
cutbank, and she sat staring with startled eyes.

"Silver Hat," she repeated incredulously, "why . . .
where is Harold?"

"Dead," he whispered. "But don't talk so loud.

Here, take a drink and see if you can walk. The Hopis are on our trail."

She raised her hand to her face as if brushing away a veil, and followed obediently after him. Then, like two wild creatures, they lay down by a pool and drank deeply.

"Why . . . how did I get here?" she asked as he raised her up. "It all seems so different . . . and strange."

"I carried you," he answered, taking her hand. "Now see if you can walk."

She stepped off weakly, then looked back up the cañon and broke into a frightened run.

"I remember now!" she gasped. "It was terrible! Terrible!"

"Then run," he urged, and they sped away down the cañon until at last she fetched up, panting.

"Where are we going?" she demanded anxiously. "This isn't the path we came."

"I know it. The Hopis have cut us off. We can never get out up the cañon so we might as well go down it and hide. My scouts will begin hunting us at dawn."

"Then come," she said, clutching his hand, and they ran until far into the night. Past the cliff dwelling where Lady Grace had been held prisoner, past cliffs that rose higher and higher, and always, when they stopped, the old fear urged her on until he marveled at her strength.

"You are strong," he said admiringly. "We have come a good ten miles and the moon is just going down."

"I am afraid," she gasped. "Oh, what terrible creatures! They had me under a spell. Everything that they told me I felt constrained to do. But something happened . . . at the end."

"You fainted," he explained briefly, "and I brought you away."

"But how did you find me?" she asked.

"Old Desteen gazed through his crystal and saw you at the cliff dwelling. You were sitting in the sun . . . with Harold. Then he prayed to the gods and shook his hand in every direction, and it guided us to the edge of this cañon. I could see you through my field glasses when you started for the dance, so I came down at dusk to bring you out. But now we're both cut off."

"I am sorry," she said contritely. "If they find us, will they kill us?"

"They'll kill me," he answered grimly, and Lady Grace understood the rest.

"I will never be taken alive," she stated. "We must run on till we drop."

With a strength that almost overmatched his own, she led the way on and on, nor did she pause until at last, quite spent, she sank down in the sand. The first flush of dawn was lighting the eastern sky, painting the bare face of the cliff with a mysterious, rosy glow, when she roused up and looked at the walls.

"Always higher and higher," she sighed. "Is there no way out of this cañon?"

"I don't know," he responded. "But no matter where we go, the Hopis will find our tracks."

"Then how can we escape them?"

"That is what I have been figuring on," he said. "Before I left the rim, I told old Desteen to look for me through his crystal. That will tell him we are still alive. Then he will try his hand-shaking, to find out where we are, and the scouts will follow on our trail."

Once more she passed her hand before her eyes as if brushing away a veil and looked up with a troubled smile.

"I seem living," she murmured, "in a different world. It is like a land of dreams. I cannot understand how this magic can be, but since it led you to where I was hidden, perhaps it will lead them to us."

She rose up wearily and took the trail down the cañon while Silver Hat, stiff with cold, plodded doggedly after her until the sun came over the rim. It found them at a marsh where the stream had widened out, and, as they passed it, he reached out and stripped a handful of seeds from a frond of leaning sedge.

"Try that," he said, stopping to gather more and more. "The Indians call it chipmunk corn."

"Why, it tastes just like nuts . . . or toast!" she exclaimed. "And, oh, how famished I am."

She ran along the edge of the sedgy grass, stripping head after head and eating it eagerly while Silver Hat filled the slack of his kilt. Then like children they sat down against a warm bank and broke their all-night fast.

"We are savages," said Grace with a rueful laugh. "Here we sit, half-naked and daubed with clay, and eat the seeds of grass. But already it has given me new strength. Perhaps, after all, I was meant for such a life, although to you it is nothing strange."

"You stand it well," he answered gravely. "We have been running most of the night. But we must still go on until this cañon ends or we find a place to hide."

He held out his hand to help her up, and, as she rose, she held it fast.

"With you," she said, "I could go anywhere . . . brave anything. I must have died. It is like a dream."

She glanced up at him meekly and they walked on, hand in hand. But as they rounded a point, a high cliff rose before them and they heard a deep, sullen roar. Their lesser cañon had come to an end in the Grand Cañon of the Colorado.

CHAPTER SEVENTEEN

The river was in flood, hurling furious red waves against the sheer cliffs that straitened its course, while in the middle smooth rollers glided and sank in oily haste as they rushed toward a black point below. Huge cottonwood logs bobbed solemnly past, angry wavelets lapped the shore, and, as Silver Hat and Lady Grace stood breathlessly in its presence, the Rio Colorado roared. Deep and terrifying, like the voice of some great monster, from the sunless abyss there came thunderous reverberations that shook the very earth beneath their feet.

"What can we do? Where can we go?" she asked, and Silver Hat shook his head.

"Nothing! Nowhere!" he answered, and turned back with ashen lips.

Between the mouth of Chua Cañon and Toh-neely, the mighty river, a wide sandbar rose up like a bulwark, and along its slope the wreckage of bridges and fences lay strewn with logs and stumps. But on the landside its sand was clean and smooth and Silver Hat dropped down to rest—and watch. Sooner or later, around the bend above, the Hopis would come running on their trail, and then, unless the scouts saved them, they would suffer a cruel death.

Lady Grace sank down beside him and gazed up into his face that was deep-lined and set, like a mask.

"Can you swim?" she asked.

"Who . . . me?" He laughed. "I've been raised in a dry country. Were you thinking of going down the river?"

"Where else can we go?" she countered, and he gazed at her in blank surprise.

"Down that cañon?" he quavered. "With those waves ten feet high? A fish couldn't hardly get through."

"But what of the Hopis?" she inquired.

"They'll kill us, sure as shooting, if Desteen doesn't come. I reckon I didn't tell you that I knifed Harold myself. And old Masawa is chief."

"Then what do you intend to do?"

"Wait here," he answered hoarsely, "and put up a fight. I'll take some of them with me to hell."

"Oh, poor Silver Hat!" she cried, laying her head against his shoulder. "And there is nothing that I can do. Before I came, you were free and happy, riding the plains and living your own life. But now, because of me, you have fallen into this trap. Your adoptive father was right."

"What do you mean?" he asked absently, looking back from watching the cañon, and she reached up and took his hand.

"He told you," she said, "to avoid women like me. Willful women, bound to have their own way. And what does it matter now if I say I am sorry? Can you ever forgive me, Silver Hat?" She clasped his hand beseechingly, but he seemed not to hear. "I know," she went on, "that we have lived different lives. And to forgive is not easy for you. But please look at me, Silver Hat, and say you do not blame me too much. I am doomed to die, too, as you know. But not at the hands of the Hopis. I am going down the river . . . alone."

"Down the river!" he cried. "Can *you* swim?"

"Yes, indeed," she answered. "And I will cling to a log. Who knows what is around the bend?"

"It's just like that," he said, "for miles and miles. But still, a man might win. What I hate the most is to face these damned Hopis with nothing but *this* in my hand."

He drew out the bloody knife and she shivered at the sight of it.

"No, not that way," she pleaded. "Their arrows are poisoned."

"If I just had my guns!" he burst out, and once more she bowed her head.

"I know," she responded soberly. "But perhaps Desteen will come. There is nothing to do but wait."

She rose up slowly and went back to the river, and, when Silver Hat looked over at a pile of driftwood, she was struggling with a log.

"Here," he cried, striding impatiently after her, "let me carry that thing down. You go back and watch for the Hopis." And he snaked the log down to the shore. Then, looking about, he picked out another one, dragged it halfway down, and stopped. From the chasm below, a thunderous roar came echoing back as the sand and mud, passing through the smooth rollers, suddenly broke their tops into spray. He stood at gaze, taking in anew the ponderous sweep of the stream, the height of the frowning cliffs, and, when he looked down, Grace was there.

"God A'mighty," he breathed, "are you going down that river? Look at those big whirlpools that can suck down a tree. What chance have you got against them?"

"Other people have passed through the Grand Cañon in boats. Why can't I go down on a log?"

He glanced at her curiously, then back at the swirling stream.

"The Navajos believe," he said at last, "that a devil lives down in those suck holes. Tayholtsodi, they call him, and they never cross the river without making him an offering of turquoise. He grabs people by the legs and pulls them down and down, and keeps them on the bottom for his slaves."

"But you don't believe that?" she cried.

"Well, maybe not . . . but I was raised with the Navajos. It looks mighty scary to me. And, besides, I can't swim a stroke."

"Just cling to a log, and hold your breath when you go under. Oh, Silver Hat, please come. It's our only chance to live. And life means so much to us now."

She clung to him appealingly, but at another terrific roar he shook his head and turned pale.

"I'm afraid," he said at last. "There's something about water . . ."

"But I'm going through!" she cried.

"I'd swallow my heart, and die, before I was wet," he answered, and turned back to the slope.

The sun was higher now and down the wide cañon the wind devils came whipping up the dust, but the whole world seemed empty as he watched, until at last Grace came and joined him.

"Perhaps," she said hopefully, "the Hopis won't come. Or perhaps your scouts will save us. We have come so far and escaped so much. . . ."

"I knew it," he growled, leaping up.

He pointed up the cañon and in the midst of a dust cloud Lady Grace saw a bobbing head. Another appeared behind it, another and another, and Silver Hat felt for his knife.

"No, no!" she cried, holding him back. "Not that way, Silver Hat . . . not filled with poisoned arrows. Not pulled down like a stag by those dogs. Let's push off with two logs before they come closer and float down the river together."

He glanced back, undecided, at the swift-flowing stream, and his cheeks became ashen as he gazed.

"I'm afraid," he muttered. "Afraid of the water. You go . . . I'll keep them back."

"No, Silver Hat," she answered quietly. "I won't leave you now. I'll stay . . . we will die together."

"But I can't swim, I tell you!" he raged. "I'd go down like a rock. There's old Masawa . . . you know what he will do to you. Go ahead, before it's too late."

"I *can't* go, Silver Hat!" she wailed. "I'm afraid, too . . . afraid to die. But if only you were with me. . . ."

"Well, come on, then!" he exclaimed. "It will soon be over. They've seen us . . . they're spreading out."

He caught her by the arm and hurried her over the driftwood logs, and, as the Hopis saw them flee, they gave a shrill yell and came charging down the cañon.

"Go to hell!" yelled back Silver Hat, whipping out his knife, but Lady Grace pulled him back.

"*Please* come, Silver Hat," she pleaded, "before it's too late. Just think, if one arrow should break your skin. . . ."

"They're afraid of me." He laughed, still brandishing his knife. "They know what I did to Harold. It will be a long time before they come over this driftwood. . . ."

"No . . . come!" she said. And Silver Hat came.

As Lady Grace sat down and unwrapped her moccasins, he dragged one of the smooth logs to the water's edge, but just as he stepped into the water, an angry wave slapped at his leg. He jumped back, cursing the river with passionate hate, and the great chasm roared in answer.

"I can't do it!" he cried as she ran down beside him. "Go ahead, if you're going . . . I'll fight it out with the Hopis!" And he turned his face resolutely away.

They were coming now, swarming over the racks of driftwood, and Lady Grace pushed out her log. Then impulsively she ran back and stood beside him, where he bristled, knife in hand.

"Good-bye, Silver Hat," she whispered. "Do you mind if I kiss you?" And slowly, reverently, she kissed him on the cheek, although the arrows were beginning to fall. Then, smiling back at him, she pushed boldly out and floated off down the stream. An arrow struck close beside him with a vicious *sput*, the Hopis set up a yell, but still he stood watching her go. Then suddenly he grabbed his log and pushed out after her, and the great river rushed him along.

CHAPTER EIGHTEEN

In the rush of surging waters that bore him on and on, Silver Hat clung desperately to his bobbing log while the high walls closed in like a tomb. They drew closer, hanging over him, but far above like a golden road he saw sunlight, and the blue sky beyond. A flight of arrows fell around him as, yelling with hate, the Hopis twanged their weak bows, but in the clutch of the mighty river Silver Hat did not even notice. He was panic-stricken—frozen with fear. But as he stared into the abyss that yawned before him, he saw Lady Grace, waving her hand.

She lay like a mermaid athwart her floating log, and like a flag, waving valiantly, her slender arm beckoned him on until she swung around the point and was gone. Then the raging torrent seized him and swept him against the cliff, where boiling waves hurled him roughly back, flinging man and log out into midstream. A millrace of turbid waters leaped and danced before him, sending up a heart-stilling roar, and once more, as he clutched and gasped, it headed him straight for a dripping wall, only to fling him back before he struck.

He went under, clinging desperately, and, when he opened his eyes, he was floating serenely along. The towering wall had given way, letting in a touch of sun and, in the midst of it, her lithe body gleaming, he saw Lady Grace, looking back. Then, swimming like an otter, she propelled her log before her until suddenly she appeared at his side.

"We will come through," she said, smiling encouragingly, but Silver Hat had forgotten how to smile. Even out in the still water he clung tightly to his log, saying nothing, staring wildly about, for already around the bend he could hear the voice of the mighty river that was shouting for his life. It sucked him in, it pulled him down, until once more the millrace seized him and rushed him relentlessly on. A red wave rose before him; he heard its booming thunder as it leaped before the cavern it had formed. Then something drew him down, like the hands of Tayholtsodi, who claims drowning men for his slaves.

He rose up gasping, spitting out the muddy water that had forced itself down his throat, and, as his weary grip relaxed, he felt a hand beneath him that laid him across his log.

"We will come through yet," said a voice in his ear, and suddenly his courage returned. He drew a sobbing breath and struck the hair from his eyes, and there was Lady Grace, smiling.

"Just lie on it and float," she advised. "The walls are not so high. Around the next point some cañon may open out. Hold fast . . . I am going ahead."

Dropping down behind her log, she thrust her feet out behind, and like the wake of a propeller he saw the water churn as she plowed down into the unknown. She waved her hand bravely, almost playfully, as if shooting the roaring rapids were a game, but before them now there lay a narrow, zigzag cañon where the leaping waves were beaten to a spray. The echoing walls rumbled to an ominous reverberation and the wet rocks gleamed in the murk. Then the water god laid hold of him and he felt his hands slip as the log was snatched away. But when he came up, it fell back into his arms again, and he closed down on it with a death grip.

Over ledges, through rapids, around rocky points he went rushing at a furious pace, now under, now on top, now gasping for breath only to draw in a mouthful of mud. The water was not water—it was liquid mud, washed down from the raging streams above, and every lock of his hair, his snake kilt, his moccasins were weighed down by a slimy deposit. The log was becoming slippery with a coating of mud, and, just as he drifted down into a whirling vortex, it leaped from his hands again. But with a last desperate plunge he laid hold of it, and toppled over into the boiling abyss.

Down, down, clinging blindly, his lungs bursting for air, he went swirling into the depths, until suddenly he rose up and went rocking gently on, although where he did not know. All his strength had left him; he could hardly raise his head, when quick hands heaved him up on another log that glided away toward the shore.

When he opened his eyes, Lady Grace was leaning over him, washing away the clinging mud with water from a sparkling stream.

"Just think!" she cried, stooping closer and kissing him. "We are safe! We have come through alive!"

He lifted his head wearily and looked about. The great river was at his feet, but behind him a narrow cañon opened out into a grassy valley. Yellow walls rose on either side, and down one, like the overflow from a fountain, a shower of spring water dripped. From shelf to shelf, among green masses of moss and ferns it fell, making rainbows in the sun, while on a knoll before them, as if completing the picture, a stone house stood like a fort.

"Someone lives here," she said. "Look at the cows."

He rose up groggily, hardly able to stand, and in a half circle around them hundreds of cattle stood at gaze. Not an ear moved as with startled eyes they stood frozen to the earth, staring in absolute silence at the two strange figures that had dragged themselves up on the shore. But when he took a step toward them, they whirled and fled until they dashed around the corner of a bend.

"There's nobody here," he answered, "or the cattle wouldn't be so wild. But let's go up to that cabin, and see what there is to eat."

He toiled up the trail, barely able to lift his moccasins, so heavily were they impregnated with mud, but now that the battle with the waters was over their old, gnawing hunger had returned. The door, made of planks, was padlocked, hard and fast, and the one window was boarded up. Lady Grace sank down wearily on the hewn-log bench that stood in front of the house, but the pangs of hunger were gripping Silver Hat's vitals and he jerked a long pole from the fence. Then, jamming it beneath the log chain, he heaved with all his strength until at last the stubborn lock gave way.

The door swung open, revealing a table and fireplace and a bed of sweet ferns on the floor, and from the rafters, suspended by wires to keep off the rats, there hung six sides of bacon and two full sacks of flour. One corner was piled high with squares of rock salt and from a cupboard against the wall Silver Hat dug out plates and dishes and a last battered can of tomatoes.

"Ah," he sighed, and, cutting the top off with his knife, he handed the brimming can to Lady Grace. They drank turn and turn about and made a meal on fried bacon and flapjacks. Then, hand in hand, they started up the cañon to see what lay around the bend. But when they rounded the point and the wide valley opened before them, all their hopes were dashed to nothing. On every side the high wall ran on endlessly. They were shut in—there was no way out.

CHAPTER NINETEEN

The walls that shut in this lost valley among the peaks rose up grandly, terrace on terrace, while at their base in a tremendous talus, huge blocks of yellow sandstone told the story of their creation. Tawny grass covered the plain and mounted up the steep slopes to the face of the 1,000-foot cliff and among the jagged rocks coarse bunches of sotol and bear grass stood out in brighter greens. But nowhere in all the wide sweep of the park was there a sign of water or a tree—the cattle that fed there came perforce to the river where they had stood when the fugitives appeared.

Lady Grace looked at Silver Hat and unloosed her hand as the gravity of their situation came over her. They had escaped from the river only to find themselves immured, shut in inexorably like the great herd of cattle in this wide, smiling valley prison. But as she gazed at the painted walls that cut them off from the world, she reached up trustingly for Silver Hat's rugged hand and drew him gently away.

They were worn out, weary with battling the treacherous river that had so nearly sucked them down, and, although the last of their hopes had been destroyed, they turned back without a word. For two days and a night they had been tossed about like puppets on the tumultuous seas of life. Death and dishonor had narrowly passed them by, and on the morrow more dangers would come. But now, sleep was closing their drooping eyes, and they returned to the sweet-fern bed.

Silver Hat divided the fragrant mass into two separate heaps and dropped down, dead to the world. When he awoke, Lady Grace was close beside him, and they were covered like babes in the woods. Her warm body lay close to his, and, as she slumbered peacefully, he could feel the soft touch of her hands. It was dawn outside and through the broken-latched door the keen morning wind sifted in, but beneath their blanket of leaves they slept on innocently, too close to Nature to care.

He lay silently, thinking, going back in lightning steps to the beginning of this madcap flight, and, as the memory of her strange, impassioned kisses came over him, he opened his eyes with a start. She had drunk of the snake chief's witch brew, the love medicine of the Mother Earth Dance! Could it be that her nature had undergone some change? Old Masawa's medicine had been strong.

In his cabin on the mountain she had been haughty, imperious, demanding as her right that all the world should serve her, oblivious of the trouble she made. While the soldiers had scoured the plains, seeking desperately to find her and rescue her from a terrible fate, she had watched them ride by until her satiny skin was healed, the better to cover up her shame. She had taken everything, given nothing, and, when he forgot, she had slapped him in the face.

But that was not the Grace who lay so trustingly beside him, who sought his hand when they walked forth together, and had kissed him as he came back to life. All fear, all maidenly shame, had been effaced from her nature—and yet she was Lady Grace. She was a Benedict, the daughter of an English earl, and some day their prison walls would part. They would escape from this valley that now shut them in. How would he make answer then? What would he say when he stood before Major Doyle, or faced the stern-eyed Lord Benedict? He inched away slowly, gently, his ears tense for any break in her breath, and, when he was free, he rose up and lit a fire. Then as the room became warm and she slept on, never stirring, he went out and closed the door.

In the great world above them the sun was shining brightly, throwing grotesque shadows along the shattered walls, illuminating the Grand Cañon below. From the black abyss of its chasm there came the echoes of the river's mighty roar, and from the corner of the house he could see the dimpling circle of the whirlpool that had sucked him down. As easily could he mount the battlemented walls as face again the terrors of that stream. He stood erect, gazing from cliff to river, pondering grimly on their fate, when from the cabin behind him Lady Grace emerged, her eyes still drowsy with sleep.

Her tangled locks were mud-stained, her body bare except for the Hopi skirt, but there was something about her bearing that still gave her dignity and enhanced the rare beauty of her form. Clothed in rags, grimed with silt, reduced to the primitive, she stepped forth like a queen of the long ago and greeted him with a smile.

"I woke up," she said, "and you were gone, and suddenly I felt afraid. But what a world for just you and me." She reached out and took his hand.

He glanced down at her curiously and started to speak, then closed his lips on the words. Since they were there, since it pleased her to hold his hand, why deny the comfort she sought? They were a man and woman alone, with no one to look on, and soon enough it would come to an end. But what end? Would they dwell on, undiscovered, until Desteen and the scouts came in over the crags above, or would some rough cattleman, the owner of the herd, come upon them by surprise? He looked back at the swift-flowing river, big and booming from the summer rains, and she read what was in his mind.

"Who could it be," she asked, "that would build a cabin here? And how could he bring in these cattle, when the river is so dangerous and high?"

"In the winter, the water will be low," he answered, and left the rest unsaid. The man who would hide in a place like that would be one of a desperate sort—an outlaw, a rustler, quick to resent their presence, unwilling to accept explanations. They had escaped the river and the malevolent Hopis, only to drop into the rendezvous of some band of cattle thieves, or worse. An old cow that stood bawling near the spring had a newly peeled and altered brand, but why poison Grace's happiness by doubts and apprehensions when she could gaze with such rapturous eyes?

"What a world," she mused dreamily, "and to think that you and I should be shut up in it, alone. With nothing but these rags and our moccasins, and yet so well content. Isn't it wonderful, after all we have been through, that at last we should catch a glimpse of paradise? I have a feeling that always we shall look back to this time . . . and perhaps with a sense of regret. But let us go up to the spring and survey our new Eden."

"I'll get me a club first," observed Silver Hat, "to drive away that cow. She acts like she's lost her calf."

He picked up an oak stave that lay by the fence that ran from the spring to the house and, with Lady Grace behind, walked slowly up the path, a rock in his other hand. But as they advanced upon the cow, she broke and fled, and he threw the stone away.

"There may be a bog hole," he suggested, "where her calf has sunk in and drowned." But as they approached the fenced-in spring, the water was clear at the long pool where the cattle drank. Over terrace after terrace of the fern-covered cliff it came dripping in crystal showers, until at last, through a thick growth of willows, it flowed forth a good-sized stream. But halfway up the trail Silver Hat stopped short and reached for a rock.

"It's a mountain lion," he whispered. "See that track in the path? You'd better go back if you're afraid."

"No, indeed," she returned, picking up a rock herself.

Silently he followed the track. Every footprint was as large as the palm of his hand, and at the edge of a thicket of scrub oaks he found the signs of the kill. There was blood on the ground, the brush was trampled down, and just across the fence among the willows he caught sight of a tawny hide. Then, with a glance at Lady Grace, he flung back his hand and hurled the rock with all his might.

"*Haahr!*" he yelled, waving his club in the air, and, just as Lady Grace smashed her rock into the bushes, the lion leaped up on a boulder. With white fangs gleaming, he glared back with a snarl at these strange creatures that had invaded his lair, but Silver Hat hit him fairly with his second stone, and the huge beast bounded away.

"Now for some beef." Silver Hat laughed, vaulting over the fence, and down through the willows he came dragging a gnawed carcass—the remains of the old cow's calf. Lady Grace danced after him as he ran back to the house, and soon, over the coals, they were broiling strips of meat to break their long-standing fast. Then at last, when they could eat no more, they went out to bask in the sun.

"I'm going to like this place," observed Silver Hat with a grin. "No man ever starved as long as he could get beef, and that lion kills a calf every day. I've followed them, lots of times, and found where they'd buried a deer and covered it up with leaves."

"Oh, Silver Hat," she said, leaning her head against his shoulder and gazing up into his eyes, "just think of robbing a lion of his prey in order to get something to eat. But all our past life has fallen away from us . . . don't you wish this could go on forever?"

"Well . . . almost," he qualified. "We've got lots of beef. But what are we going to do when our flour runs out? It won't last very long."

"Right over that fence, where the cows haven't

been, I saw some chipmunk corn. Let's go up and gather some and grind it between two rocks, the way the Indians do."

"After a while," he agreed lazily. "And while we're up there, we can wash some of the silt out of our hair."

"Oh, wonderful," she sighed. "I saw such a shower bath, where the water flows over a ledge. And then, if we have time, we can pluck some ferns and grass and make two nice, big beds."

"We'll do that first," he responded soberly, and Lady Grace glanced up shyly.

"Did you mind," she asked, "when I moved over closer? I was so tired and sleepy, but I was shivering with cold. And then it was so nice and warm."

"I didn't know you were there," he answered. "But now that we're going to be here a while, we'd better fix up our house. I'll lay a fire tonight and fasten the door tight, and maybe that will keep out the cold."

"Isn't there something," she demanded, "that we can make into blankets? This man who owned our cabin must have lived like a big mouse, all huddled up in his nest."

"He took his blankets away when he left," replied Silver Hat. "But we can sleep like mice, for a while. After we're settled down, I'll kill a yearling and maybe we can tan the hide. How'd you like a suit of clothes?"

"Oh, Silver Hat," she protested, laughing, "must we make everything that we had back at the fort? We can find some white clay, such as the Indians use, and daub our skins to keep out the cold. And you look so straight and strong, with nothing on but your kilt. Couldn't we go back to Nature for a time?"

"We're back there right now," responded Silver Hat, and stretched his naked arms to the sun.

"Does it distress you," she asked anxiously, "to see me the way I am? You're such a grim soul. I never can tell what is going on in your mind."

He looked far away at the towering cliffs and down at the rushing stream, then he took the tender hand that was clinging to his and pressed it against his heart.

"Not a bit," he said bluffly. "You're just the way God made you."

"And you," she said gravely, "are made in His image. So beautiful, so daring, so good . . . what a pity it must come to an end."

Silver Hat stirred uneasily and put her hand away.

"I wonder how it will end," he said.

CHAPTER TWENTY

Beneath the dripping overhang of the fern-clad cliff, in a pool the storm waters had dug, Lady Grace splashed about with the joyous freedom of a nymph while her damp skirt hung in the sun. Down below, Silver Hat had dug up a sotol, and, using the pounded roots for soap, he was washing the silt from his hair. Then he scrubbed out the dirt from the Hopi kilt he wore and sat in the sun to dry. He felt clean and strangely pure, resigned to his fate, unafraid of what the future held in store. At a call from above he made his way through the bushes where she sat, drying her hair.

Delicate fronds of maidenhair ferns and sweet-smelling bracken made a couch half hidden from the sun, and, as she glanced up smilingly, she fluffed out her golden locks and stretched her slender limbs luxuriously.

"It is so beautiful here," she sighed, "so fragrant and peaceful. Who would think that only yesterday we were fleeing for our lives, or floundering in the muddy river? But sit down here, Silver Hat, and we will never speak of all that again. It is something that is best forgotten."

She made room close beside her, and he sat down, still-faced, in the presence of a beauty that awed him. Beneath the golden cataract of her tumbled hair she seemed more than a woman—a siren, yet innocent and unafraid. There was nothing to remind him of the haughty Lady Grace as she reached out and took his hand.

"I am afraid," she said, "when you leave me alone. For what would I do if the great lion should come while my natural protector is away? We have gone back to Nature, almost as naked as the day we were born, in this land of wild animals and wild men. There is something about it that makes me feel very humble . . . I need you, dear Silver Hat, very much. And since you have saved me from . . . *them*, I feel as if I were yours. Like poor Jani, who gave you his secret name. It will be hard, I know, for I am naturally willful, but as long as we are lost here together I shall try to do what you say."

She glanced out wistfully from the canopy of her flowing hair and took her clinging hand away.

"I have been thinking it over," she went on soberly, "and, until we escape, we must live like the cavemen who dwelt in these ancient cliffs. I must do the woman's work . . . picking the seeds, grinding the meal, preparing the food . . . while you stand guard over me and bring in game and meat. Would you like it that way, Silver Hat?"

"Suits me," he answered briefly, but he did not meet her eyes.

"Why is it," she asked, "that you always watch the

river? Are you afraid that someone will come?"

"Yes," he replied. "I'm afraid of these cattlemen. They've lost lots of calves, on account of this old lion that is skulking around the water hole. The cows have to come here to drink, and, of course, he catches their calves, but the cowmen will blame it on me. And then, if we stay here long, we will have to kill some more . . . and we haven't a cent to pay for it."

"But we can tell them," she protested, "who I am, and *Pater* will pay them well."

"That would be fine," he conceded, "if we could just get them to listen. But here I am, with nothing but a knife if they happen to pull a gun. So, if anyone comes, I want you to hide until we have had our talk."

She straightened up quickly, a fighting fire in her eyes.

"You want me to run," she repeated, "and leave you to face them alone?"

"That's the idea." He nodded. "It will be safer for both of us. And remember now . . . I'm the boss! When I tell you to do something, I want you to do it. We can talk the matter over afterwards."

He smiled at her grimly, and Lady Grace bowed her head.

"Very well," she said, "you know best."

"But no one will come," he added, "as long as the water is high. And before the rains stop, I look for old Desteen to come in over the cliffs. Being a Navajo, he'll never try the river."

"But tell me, Silver Hat," she pleaded, "about this stargazing. I was so distraught when you mentioned it yesterday that I just couldn't understand. Is it really something dependable? Do you think they can find us . . . here?"

"They can find us anywhere," he answered confidently. "That is, if the medicine works. The conditions have got to be right . . . perfect silence, everyone in accord . . . but for all we know, Desteen may see us right now."

"Then we ought to smile," she said, "to show how happy we are, while we are waiting to be saved."

"I don't know," he responded darkly. "If the old man saw us now, he might think we didn't want to be saved."

"Why, Silver Hat," she chided, drawing away the slender hand that would creep out to his, and then she heaved a sigh. "Can he read our thoughts?" she asked.

"I don't doubt it," he replied. "Old Desteen can do anything when his medicine is working fine. He can see visions, interpret dreams, and, when he looks right through you, he can tell how long you will live. If your body is all light inside, you will live a long time. If it is dark halfway up, not so long. If the light is up on top of your head, you will die in twenty-four hours."

"Really?" she asked. "Do you believe it?"

"It works for the Navajos," he evaded. "And I reckon I'm mostly Indian by this time. I've lived with them all my life."

"And do you like it?" she queried eagerly.

"Yes, I do," he answered. "It's the only life for me. If I had to stay in a town, I'd die."

"And you do like this, right now . . . you and I sitting together, the only man and woman in our world? Would you care if old Desteen should peep in and find us happy, and do nothing for months and months? Then I'm going to make signs for the scouts to go away." Impulsively she leaped out into the sun.

She stood erect, facing the east, and raised her hands toward the cliffs, then gracefully she waved their rescuers away, and came back with a mischievous smile.

"So, there!" she said. "When your grandfather sees that . . ."

"He'll think we're crazy," he ended.

"Then I'll let him see this." She laughed, and kissed him lightly on the cheek. "Do Navajos kiss?" she asked.

"I don't know," he confessed. "I've seen them kissing their babies, but . . ."

"And would you rather," she suggested, "that I wouldn't kiss you any more? You're almost an Indian, you know."

"Well . . . ," he began, and then he stopped and took her hand in his. "As long as it's all right with you," he said, "I reckon it's all right with me."

"Yes, yes, Silver Hat," she answered, looking up with glowing eyes. "I know you're the best man in the world. But something has come over me . . . I don't know exactly what it is. I never liked kisses before."

"I'm not used to them myself," he said at last, and at some memory she drew her arms away.

"Yes, Silver Hat," she said. "I will try to remember. We must not break up our new paradise."

CHAPTER TWENTY-ONE

A pile of gleaming thunderheads appeared suddenly over the rim as Silver Hat and Lady Grace, their arms full of ferns, staggered down from their hanging garden. Within its dank caverns the air had been warm and moist, like the atmosphere of a summer greenhouse, but outside in the smiting sun the heat radiated from the cliffs in quivering waves of light. Lightning flashed from the sagging belly of the cloud, a mutter of thunder came from the heights, and then with a roar a squall of wind swept up the cañon and broke against their house. Sand flew, sticks danced about, until suddenly there was an ominous pause.

From the window they could see a seething black wall come rolling and tumbling up the gorge. It spread out, torn to tatters, dragging dark trailers behind it, until with a thunderous cannonade it struck against the face of the cliff. Then the rain came pouring down, the day turned black as night, and the earth shook beneath a blinding stroke. The next minute the clouds were gone, the sun came rolling out, and from top to bottom the lofty crag about them was turned into a sparkling waterfall.

Silver Hat glanced at Grace as they stood outside the door and gazed up at the iridescent rainbow.

"It's a dry country," he said, "but I begin to understand where all that spring water comes from. Every time a cloud blows against the cliff, it turns loose everything right there."

"But it's all so beautiful, when it's over," she murmured. "What a place to spend one's life. We never know what is going on above us in that great world that's open to the sky, and then, up the river or over some crag a storm comes that shakes the earth. It is like life itself . . . like our life together, Silver Hat. I hope it ends as beautifully."

She stood beside him silently, gazing up at the gorgeous spectacle of 1,000 feet of waterfall bathed in fire, but, although her eyes grew big and she looked up at him often, she did not take his hand. Like the rain, her first stormy passion had passed and they had entered a period of calm. There were so many things to do to make their house habitable, but all the time as she worked at his side her face wore a dreamy smile.

Piling the great blocks of rock salt into a wall between them they made new beds of dry grass and ferns and hurried on to other tasks. With a broom of willow twigs Grace swept the dusty floor and scoured the grimy saucepans with sand. Then she cleaned all the dishes and set them in order and counted the matches in their can. There were less than two blocks of the queer sulphur matches that ran 100 to the square, and, when they were gone,

Silver Hat would have to make fire sticks or improvise a flint-and-steel. But of salt there was plenty and to spare, and Silver Hat pounded up a chunk to cure his beef.

Then, cutting the meat in strips, he rubbed it in thoroughly and hung the jerky out to dry. But suddenly as they worked the light grew dim—the sun had gone down before its time. Far above them on the high mesa the day still went on, but down in their narrow cañon the twilight had set in and night was on its way. They brought in wood and water, cooked a meal in the corner fireplace, and then the day was done. A long day full of excitements and tempestuous emotions that had left them weary and spent, and, after sitting by the fire, they rose up in silence and crept into their fragrant beds.

For hours the stored-up heat of the sun was radiated by the thick stone walls, and then, as the chill night air crept in, they burrowed deeper and deeper into their ferns. Silver Hat rose at last and started a fresh fire, using up another precious match, and, when the sky began to lighten, he stepped out the door and gazed up at the paling stars. It was strange, it was beautiful, this lost valley among the crags, but it was a prison, after all. From the black gorge of the cañon a cold wind drew in that struck to the marrow of his bones. He was naked, and in her bed Lady Grace was beginning to shiver—that was why he had come outdoors.

How long, he asked himself, could this life go on? For in some such stormy time his fortitude might desert him—she was not like other women. Every touch of her dainty hands, every glance of her smiling eyes, roused something within him that made his senses reel and filled him with surging desires. The subtle magic of old Masawa's love potion had passed from her veins to his, but their dreams could never come true. She was still Lady Grace, the daughter of an earl, and he was a plain government scout, a white man whose given name at birth had been Milton Buckmaster but who had been raised as a Navajo. With sudden resolution he began dragging up logs—it was time for the signal fire.

Just at dawn, when the cañon winds blew neither up nor down and all the upper air was calm, Desteen would be watching for the puffs of smoke that would guide him to their valley. The cliffs were high, but they could be scaled—the soldiers would come to their aid, and, when it was over and she was gone, he could resume his carefree life. She would go back to England, to the Lionel she had forgotten, and all he would have was a dream.

Heaving mightily, he set one log against another, upended to the sky, and laid dry wood beneath, but, when he opened the door to bring out coals, he found Lady Grace by the fire.

"What is it, Silver Hat?" she asked, and her gentle voice thrilled him. "Did you, too, find it cold? When the sun is warm and bright, we can talk of back to Nature, but at night one thinks of clothes."

"Yes, we do," he said, "and, as soon as it is day, I am going to kill a yearling. Then we'll tan the skin and make you a tunic, like the one you had before."

"Dear Silver Hat." She smiled up at him. "I have never even thanked you for the beautiful buckskin suit you gave me, and yet you are planning for another one. But where are you going with the coals?"

"Outside," he answered, "to make a big fire. I am going to signal Desteen."

She glanced up quickly and he saw her face change, but she only bowed her head.

"Very well . . . if you think it best," she said.

"It's got to be done," he stated truculently. "The last thing I told him when I started down the trail was to look out for my smoke . . . and every morning at daylight, and just before dark, the old man will be watching the sky. But all the hand-shaking and crystal-gazing in the world would never find us here. We're buried, a thousand feet deep! Don't you feel yourself shut in?"

"No, Silver Hat," she sighed, "for me it is different. All the world is shut out . . . all the madness we call life. But if you wish to end it now, light your fire."

He gazed at her curiously, the coals losing their heat until he threw them back in the fire.

"Do you like to be cold?" he asked. "Do you like to eat straight beef and sleep like a mouse . . . only, of course, not half as warm? Do you like to be afraid that some mountain lion will get you, or some outlawed, renegade cattle thief? Do you . . . ?"

"Yes, Silver Hat," she said, "I do. I don't know why, but never in my life have I been so happy as here. Perhaps I was born to live in some far valley as my ancestors did for centuries . . . always in danger of war and enemy raids, but brave and ready to fight. They were warriors, every one."

"Well, what are we going to do when the grub runs out?" he demanded, shifting his ground. "And in a couple of months the river will go down and these men will come back for their cows. There's going to be hell to pay if they catch us here in this house."

"I understand, Silver Hat," she responded at last, "you don't need to say any more. It is I you are afraid of, not the cattle thieves and outlaws. So go out and light your fire."

He squatted down, frowning, raking out the fresh coals—then he threw them back and stood up.

"You don't know me!" he said hoarsely. "*You* ought to be afraid. Do you still think I'm a man of iron? If you'll think back a ways to the time you slapped my face . . ."

"Yes, Silver Hat," she interposed, "I remember it well. So go and light your fire, before the coals die out. And I promise never to touch you again."

He swayed on his feet, his naked breast swelling with emotions too long pent up.

"You'll have to do more than that," he said. "You'll have to put on some clothes. You're too damned beautiful . . . I can't look at you . . . you make me crazy! My God, I'm crazy already!"

"No, you're not, Silver Hat," she answered evenly. "You're a good man . . . I'll never forget. And now let's each take a pan of coals and set the signal fire."

She leaped up quickly and, seizing a blazing brand, ran out and thrust it under the pyre. Then, as the flames rose higher in the still morning air, she helped pile on the green willow boughs. The white smoke rose in billows along the face of the cliff till it reached the uttermost rim, but, as it poured over the top, Silver Hat sprang forward suddenly and beat out the roaring flame.

"What's to prevent those cow thieves from seeing it, too?" he yelled.

Lady Grace only smiled.

CHAPTER TWENTY-TWO

All day, half in sun, half in shade, Lady Grace sewed on her tunic. She had cut the winding tops from her buckskin moccasins and Silver Hat had loaned her his knife. The same keen point that had stabbed Polinuivah now served to pierce rows of holes, and thongs from the edge took the place of sinews as the soft, white garment took form. Silver Hat worked at other things, twisting the slim leaves of sotols into a mat that was to hang between their beds, and, all the time she sewed, the lady smiled. He had found her too beautiful to look upon—and the signal fire was out.

With artful care she draped the buckskin over her body and sewed the long strips into place, while for a pattern she remembered that other tunic that she had made in his mountain cabin. Through long days of suffering she had fitted and pieced until every bit was photographed on her mind, but into this one she wove nothing but happy thoughts, for she had won back the lover she had lost. Even the insult of that slap in the face had been forgotten and once more he found her beautiful.

As the chill of evening came on and they sat by the fire, she rose up silently and, behind the sotol curtain, pulled the finished garment over her head. Then with a last, anxious tug she stepped out into the light and stood waiting for his approval. Draped straight from the shoulders, leaving her slender arms bare, it descended in curved lines, artfully fitted to her figure, but, as he surveyed it, his eyes remained grim.

"Why, what's the matter," she cried, "doesn't it fit?" And for the first time he essayed a smile.

"That's the trouble," he said. "But who would think a pair of moccasins would make a dress like that?"

She looked away, blushing as she caught the implication, and then she, too, ventured to smile. "I only asked you," she explained, "because here, as on the mountain, we unfortunately have no mirror."

"You can look in the pool tomorrow," he suggested, and she sank down against the wall by the fire.

With simple directness the builder of their house had laid his raised fireplace in a corner, while above it, to carry off the smoke, he had made a chimney of wattles, daubed with mud. So, on opposite sides, they sat leaning against the wall while Silver Hat plaited another mat. Lady Grace watched him curiously, nestled down in the bed of ferns that served her for both a covering and a seat, and at last she broke the silence.

"Who showed you," she asked, "how to take

those spine-tipped leaves and make them into a mat? That is supposed to be woman's work."

"I learned it from the Indians," he said.

"Yes, but which Indians, Silver Hat? You seem to know so many. And how many languages do you speak?"

"Well . . . four. And a little Ute."

"English, Spanish, Navajo, and Hopi. Then how do you talk with the Apaches?"

"They speak the same language as the Navajos."

"And you speak such good English!" she exclaimed. "Only yesterday I heard you say 'accord'."

"What's the matter with that?" he inquired, and Lady Grace burst out laughing.

"You're trying to evade me," she charged. "But I warn you I've all night to talk. Who was it," she coaxed, "that taught you such perfect speech? Was it Grainger, your adoptive father?"

His keen eyes glanced up and returned to their work.

"Why do you want to know?" he asked.

"Because I'm interested . . . in you," she confessed. "Don't you ever wonder who I am?"

"Nope," he answered. "That isn't considered polite out here. There's some of us on the dodge."

"Oh, but surely not you, Silver Hat. Please tell me about Mister Grainger, and how he came to adopt you."

"And if I do, will you promise not to talk at the fort . . . not to tell anything till you get back to England?"

"Why . . . yes," she faltered, "if I ever get back. We're shut up in this cañon, you know."

"We'll get out," he said, and sat silently a while, thinking.

"I was lost," he began at last, "on a plain so big it didn't seem to have any end. That's all I know, except that the Indians had killed all the rest of my people. Then, away over to the east, I saw a man coming toward me. It was Selah Grainger, my new father. He picked me up and carried me a while and we came to a camp of Cheyennes. They were friendly at that time and we stayed for several months, until a white man came in sight. Then the old man grabbed me up and headed west . . . and so on, until we got out here. It took us a year or so, I reckon, but never in all that time did a white man enter our camp. My father had two pistols and a long-range rifle, and, if they didn't turn back, he'd shoot."

"Was he afraid of them?" she asked.

"Afraid of nothing," he retorted. "He'd had trouble, back East, and he knew the officers were after him. That's why, for ten years, I never saw a white man. We hid out among the Indians. Old Desteen was our friend . . . and all the other Navajos . . . until they got into trouble, too. The soldiers came in and rounded up the whole tribe and took them away to Fort Sumner, so we moved west and lived with the Hopis. I never did like the Judas-faced rascals, but they'd do anything for a box of cartridges. Yes, that's the way we made ourselves welcome . . . we sold ammunition to the Indians."

"And why not?" she inquired at last.

"Well, they'd use it to fight the white people . . . robbing wagon trains and work like that."

"Why, Silver Hat!" she exclaimed. "I wouldn't think you'd do that."

"Do anything," he said recklessly. "I was raised an outlaw. But one time the old man heard a band of Apaches making plans to raid a settlement and he sent me in to the fort. The commanding officer wouldn't believe what I told him, and about forty people were killed. Well, the next time I went in, he listened ... that's how come I'm a government scout. A hundred dollars a month, whether I work or not ... and I've never taken an order yet."

"Why, what a man," she gasped. "And I thought you were so gentle and polite."

"You can be all that," he replied, "without bowing the knee. But a man is just a dog that will salute these Army officers or flunky around to some earl."

"Silver Hat," she cried, "do you mean what you say? Have you no respect at all for rank?"

"Not a bit," he declared. "We're born free and equal. I'm as good a man as any of them."

"Then the fact that I'm a lady meant nothing to you when we first met, back at the fort?"

"No, ma'am," he answered firmly. "My father taught me to respect all good women, and to protect them as a gentleman with my life ... but out in this country the only lady is one who acts the part."

"Do you mean ... ?" she began, and stopped short. "I hope you respect *me*, Silver Hat?"

"Yes," he said, "but not as a lady. I respect you as a woman."

"A good woman?" she asked with a smile. "As I remember, your father divided women into two classes ... on account of some unpleasant circumstance."

"A woman ruined his life," he responded shortly. "That is why he warned me to avoid ..."

"Willful creatures like me?" she prompted, and Silver Hat nodded his head.

"That's what he told me," he said.

"And when we leave here, if we do," she began, "do you intend to follow his advice? Don't answer unless you wish to . . . we are shut in together . . . but I wonder what is in your mind."

"And I wonder," he countered, "what is in your mind. Do you respect me as a gentleman, or do you, being a lady . . . ?"

"I respect you as a gentleman," she stated, but Silver Hat did not make his reply. "How could I do less," she went on musingly, "when you have shown it in every act? I have never known you, Silver Hat, to be anything less than kind . . . I can't say as much for myself. But why have you never told me of this hatred you have toward people of my class?"

"Because," he responded, "we are born what we are. All I know is my birth name, Milton Buckmaster, and that out on the prairie Selah Grainger adopted me as his son. You are no more responsible for being the daughter of an earl. . . ."

"Is it any disgrace?" she cried.

"It is nothing . . . to me," he answered. "I judge you by what you are."

"And what am I?" she inquired, smiling archly. "Have I been on trial, all the time?"

"While we are in this valley," he replied, "you are a woman . . . I am a man. I am bound to protect you . . . and get you out if I can. And you are bound to do what I say, and not talk back to the boss."

He leaned back, grinning, but, as she surveyed his muscled arms and the Bowie knife in his kilt, she realized it was not all a jest. He, a simple government scout, was her master in very truth, by virtue of his ability to fight—but she could not let it lie.

"In other words," she said, "our positions are reversed. You are the lord and I am the servant. When you speak, it is my duty to obey."

"That's the idea," he agreed, "or would be, back in England. But out here we have no lords or ladies. All men and women are equal . . . there is no such thing as a servant."

"How fortunate for me," she murmured sarcastically, and Silver Hat nodded grimly.

"So you make me your equal!" she cried, flaring up, and then of a sudden she was calm. "Why not," she observed, "since we are back in the Stone Age? That steel knife . . . and you . . . is all that stands between me and the dangers of a ruthless world. But after we are out . . . what then?"

"Then you are Lady Grace and I am Silver Hat. Everything will be the same as before."

"Ah, but how was it then?" she flashed back quickly as she detected a gleam in his eye. "Did you ever consider yourself my inferior?"

"Never did." And his eyes gleamed again.

"You mean," she exclaimed incredulously, "you considered yourself better?"

"Well, think it over," he suggested. "And don't forget when you slapped my face."

She rose up, her face pale with anger, then, as she met his level glance, she settled back against the wall. She had torn aside the mask and he stood before her, as relentless as a nemesis. He judged her by what she was—rank and title were nothing. And so with beauty, wit, and charm. He was grim, inexorable—and how could she answer for that slap in the face she had given? She bowed her head at last, and, down the new tunic, a tear splashed unnoticed to the floor.

CHAPTER TWENTY-THREE

Far into the black night, while the cattle slipped in to drink and Silver Hat slept, Lady Grace lay staring into nothingness, her mind in a whirl of thought. Why had she, when all was well and his devotion so perfect—why had she persisted in questioning Silver Hat, in prying into his past? He had been quiet, reticent, without curiosity regarding her family life, and yet, in his heart, he scorned her noble blood—he cared nothing for rank or birth. All women, to him, were ladies by what they did—and no lady would slap a man's face.

It was that, by implication, which he had conveyed, although ever so delicately, when her questioning had gone too far, and suddenly there appeared before her the rankling wound that her unjust blow had left. But how, locked in his arms, overcome with passionate kisses, could she have escaped from the net she had spread? She had invited him, against his will, to cast aside the veil that until then had been set between them. She had made the

first approach, invited the first kiss, led him on until
it was too late. Yet how, having done so, could she
escape the consequences of that act? How else than
by striking back?

Over and over, in swift, rebellious thoughts that
came to nothing and had no end, she lay sighing in
her bed of dried grass and ferns while Silver Hat
was rapt in sleep. It was nothing to him that he had
wounded her to the heart, piling Pelion upon Ossa,
one slight upon the other, until at last he had told
her the truth. In all the days when his deference had
been so perfect, when her will had been his law and
he had waited upon her tenderly—in all those days
he had never for a moment considered her better
than himself. He had never recognized the lines of
caste and station that set them so far apart. In his
naïve soul he had judged her by what she was—and
in the end she had been found wanting. She had
even seemed to him less a lady than he was a
gentleman—and he an uncouth free scout!

She ran back in her mind, seeking any other in-
stance when she had been less than a gracious lady.
It all went back to that one unhappy moment when
she had repulsed him with a slap. And never, not
even when they looked death in the face, had he
granted her forgiveness for that act. When the Hopis
were upon them and the rushing river behind, and
she had kissed him a last farewell—even then he
had gazed away grimly, with the words locked behind his lips.

She sighed again, and, as she listened to his
breathing, her heart stopped at a sudden thought.
Here was no Sir Galahad, sleeping gently beside
her—he was an outlaw, a man of war, scarred in bat-

tles with the Indians—a man to whom authority meant nothing. But how far she had tempted him, in that first ecstasy of escape when some impulse drew her constantly toward him. She had laid her head trustingly on the bosom of a man to whom law and society meant nothing.* Only his strange code of honor had saved her—the teachings of the murderer, Selah Grainger.

Once again the vision of her indiscretions swept over her, when she had clung to his rough hand, laid her body against his, drawn his head down to demand a kiss. Yet always his code had held in restraint the wild passions of his lawless blood. He was a gentleman at heart, trained to respect all good women, taught to defend their honor with his life. And so he had done with her—but, when she had questioned him, she had found one disquieting thought. He had never forgiven that rude, impulsive slap with which she had met his first kiss. Would he ever forgive—ever forget?

Exhausted and distrait, she fell at last into a deep sleep that seemed of but a moment's duration. She roused up, gasping with fear, for against the door of their cabin there had come a resounding *thump*. A battle was being fought, hundreds of feet went rushing past, and above the sudden clamor of bellowing cattle she heard a heart-stilling roar. Then the agonizing bawl of a calf reached her ears and the deep, throaty snarl of a lion.

Silver Hat was up and at the door, and, as she huddled beside him, she felt the cold touch of steel.

"It's nothing but that lion," he said, his voice grating. "I thought, by the gods, those cattlemen had jumped us." And he heaved a tremulous sigh.

But now, outside the cabin, another voice had joined in—the loud, challenging bellow of a cow, the answering yowl of the lion. Then they closed in a desperate conflict and Silver Hat had opened the door as the battle moved rapidly away. In the dim light of early dawn they could see the angry mountain lion crouching defiantly over his prey, while the maddened mother struck wickedly with her horns, and he answered with savage blows. Then suddenly, lashing his tail, he launched himself upon her and she caught him on the point of one horn. Down he went, trampled and prodded, until with lightning quickness he turned over and bit into her neck. That ended the battle in an instant, and Silver Hat closed the door. He stirred up the fire, throwing on a wisp of grass, and Lady Grace stared at him wonderingly. In the bright flash of the flame his eyes were big and shining—every muscle in his body atremble.

"Do you think," she asked at last, "that the cattlemen will come like this? Oh, Silver Hat . . . and I felt so safe."

"Well, you are," he answered. "It was just that cursed lion, killing his beef in front of our door. I was up and had my knife out before I was half awake, and by the gods I'm trembling yet."

He shrugged his shoulders impatiently and piled on more wood.

"It's cold," he said at last.

"It's more than that," she sighed, creeping into his arms. "I'm afraid, Silver Hat. I'm afraid."

"You don't need to be," he responded reassuringly. "I'll take care of you . . . leave it to me."

"And I'm sorry," she rushed on impulsively, "I'm sorry I slapped you, Silver Hat."

"Oh, that's all right," he said, holding her closer, and she looked up at him, hopeful, eager.

"Do you forgive me?" she entreated. "Can you forgive me, Silver Hat? I didn't understand."

He gazed down at her, suddenly grim—then he nodded his head and she leaped up to kiss him like a child.

"I'm so glad . . . so happy." She beamed, dancing away from him, and he chuckled to himself.

"You're always glad and happy," he said. "Now go on back to bed."

"But what are *you* going to do?" she insisted as he sat down and picked up his sotol. "Are you going to finish your mat?"

"No, I'm going to make a rope to snare that old lion that gave us such a fright. This is getting too rank . . . I'm going to set a twitch-up, wherever he buries that meat."

"But you won't get hurt, Silver Hat? You won't let him kill you while you're up there setting your trap? I don't know what would happen if I were left without you . . . it seems as if I can't do anything."

"No, I'll be all right," he answered. "I'll twist a good, strong rope while he's getting his belly full of meat. Then he'll crawl away off and go to sleep."

"Let me help you," she offered, sitting eagerly down beside him. "I lay awake all night, trying to bring myself to hate you. And then we kissed and made up."

"*You* kissed!" he corrected gently. "I had nothing to do with it."

"But we're friends . . . aren't we, Silver Hat? You like me?"

"That's the trouble," he said. "I like you too much."

"Oh, Silver Hat, dear, you're so honest in what you say. And I'm never, never going to make you unhappy again. Do you wish me to go away?"

"Yes," he said smilingly, "but only over there, where you belong. And don't talk to me now, while I start this eight-ply rope. It has got to hold a lion."

She lingered over him reluctantly, watching the new rope take form, looking down at his dark, immobile face, then with a sigh she returned to her own place by the fire and almost instantly was fast asleep. He glanced across at her somberly as, leaning against the wall, she nodded in the heat of the fire, but only when her tired eyes were closed did his tense features relax in a smile.

CHAPTER TWENTY-FOUR

The lion had buried his prey in a clump of oaks, and, trimming a sapling, Silver Hat bent it over and fastened his rope to the tip. Then, while Grace held it down, he tied a toggle above the loop and hooked it into a notch and under a stick. When the trigger stick was touched, the spread loop would be twitched up, snaring the lion around the neck.

They finished their work in silence, just as the sun was coming up, and retired to the cabin to wait, but as the long day wore on and no sound came from the oaks, Lady Grace claimed her privilege to speak. Silver Hat was sitting on the bench against the warm wall of the house, lazily taking his ease after jerking the beef that the lion had left in his wake. His brawny arms were bare, his body naked to the waist, and she gazed at him admiringly.

"When you kill the lion," she said, "you must make a mantle from his skin, such as the ancient Hercules wore."

"All right," he agreed. "I suppose, if he was on the job, he would kill them with his bare hands."

"Why, Silver Hat," she exclaimed, "have you read about Hercules, and how he killed the Nemean lion?"

"Sure have," he replied. "The old man had lots of books."

"But I didn't see any," she objected.

"Oh, he had other cabins," he explained. "He kept his books in the White Mountains."

"But why so many houses?" she persisted, and he hesitated before he answered. It was such leading questions that had brought on their late misunderstanding, but at last he went on indulgently.

"Well, all trappers do that . . . they have a string of cabins just like they have strings of traps. When one range is trapped out, they go on to another. The old man was always on the move."

"But on what did he live, then?" she asked.

"He bought furs from the Indians and traded them in. And then, every year, he received a big package of money. He had some estate, back East."

"And did he leave it to you, when he died?"

"He left me the money and the string of cabins. I haven't claimed the estate."

"I don't suppose," she ventured, "you even know where it is."

"Oh, yes," he answered. "A lawyer wrote me all about it. But I was busy chasing Hopis . . . and I didn't need it, anyhow . . . so I never answered the letter."

She straightened up on the broad bench and stared at him incredulously.

"Didn't you want it?" she asked at last, and he shrugged his shoulders evasively.

"Not bad enough to go back and claim it," he replied. "They'd've kept me there for months."

"But I thought you told me last night you received only a hundred dollars a month?"

"Oh, that's just for being a scout. I give it to Jani and the boys. I can't understand," he went on, "why old Desteen doesn't come."

He glanced off up the cañon where in the evening light the lofty cliffs gleamed in the sun, but Lady Grace was not to be diverted. Each question that she asked brought up another question that piqued her curiosity even more.

"Do you mean to say seriously," she demanded, "that you care nothing for that vast estate? Just think of the income it would bring."

"But I don't need any income," he defended. "I've got the finest horse in the Territory of Arizona, the best pistols and guns, the best hat. What more could I buy if I had a million dollars? And here I am, without a shirt."

He laughed, glancing down at his half-naked body, and Lady Grace clasped her hands in dismay.

"And to think," she said, "when I left your cabin, I said my father would reward you . . . bountifully."

"Yes," he agreed, smiling bitterly. "That sure was rubbing it in."

"But you don't hold it against me, Silver Hat? I thought, of course, you were poor."

"Poor or rich," he answered, "I wouldn't have touched a cent of it. But say, let's forget all that. You can believe it or not, I rode halfway to old Mexico so I'd be sure never to see you again."

She gazed up at him reproachfully, then her eyes suddenly softened and she took his hand in hers.

"And then," she went on, "you rode all the way back, to save me from Harold and . . . that. . . . And now, here we are, shut up together. Doesn't it make you believe in fate?"

"I don't know," he said at last. "I'll tell you later on, when we see how it all comes out."

"You mean," she said, "that, when we are free, perhaps all our feelings will change? That, once we have escaped, I may forget all your kindness, and what you have suffered for my sake? Then, listen, Silver Hat . . . I am yours, like poor Jani, who your father saved from the Hopis. I, too, will give you a secret name, and, whenever you speak it, everything that I have is yours."

She leaned over impulsively and whispered in his ear, and Silver Hat nodded with a slow, brooding smile. Then he sat in the sun, his gaze far away, while he pondered on his reply.

"I thank you, my friend," he said at last, expressing his thoughts like an Indian, "for giving me your secret name. But as long as we are here in this valley, I will never speak that name."

He took her hand in his and regarded her intently, and, as they sat there in silence, the sun passed behind the rim, bringing the twilight before its time.

"This is a rough country," he went on, "and a rough life, and we are shut up together in this cañon. But when we escape, you will be free."

"I am free now," she answered, but he shook his head, then leaped suddenly to his feet. The still air was rent by a wild, strangulated outcry, and he bounded around the corner of the house.

"It's the lion!" he yelled as she followed. "Get your club . . . and keep behind."

In the clump of scrub oaks the trees bowed and swayed while in their midst, snarling and spitting, an immense, tawny form fought against the upward pull of the sapling. The big lion was snared, but, as Silver Hat rushed up, it snatched one foreleg free. Then, clawing and biting, it laid hold of the slender rope that had jerked tightly behind its ears. There was a rending tear, a strand of sotol snapped, but with a lightning leap Silver Hat sprang among the trees and struck out with all his strength. As the heavy club landed fully on its head, the struggling lion fell free.

Silver Hat dodged quickly back as the half-stunned creature crouched. Then with a mighty roar the lion sprang straight at him, and he leaped aside to avoid its claws.

"Get back!" he yelled as a slender form darted in, but as the lion landed in the open, Lady Grace ran in with her club. It struck the monster full on the nose, knocking him back in a quivering heap, and with a leap too swift to be seen Silver Hat was on him with his knife. The shining blade lunged viciously, he dodged a snarling blow, and, catching up Grace as he fled, he ran back toward the house. There, trembling with excitement, they stood in the doorway and listened till the hoarse growling ceased.

"He's dead," he said at last. "But I thought I told you to keep back."

"Yes, I know," she quavered. "But I was afraid he would kill you."

"Not as long as I could keep away from his claws. But when you ran in, I had to use my knife. He might have hooked me then."

He went back boldly and, seizing the lion by the tail, dragged the body out of the bushes while Lady Grace looked on fearfully. The huge claws twitched convulsively, the flanks heaved in a final gasp, and the monarch of the cañon was dead. With swift, skillful strokes he began stripping off the tawny hide that was to make his mantle of Hercules, and then he laid down his knife.

"You sure knocked him cold," he observed. "That's what comes from fighting blood."

"Oh, Silver Hat," she sobbed, kneeling down by the bloody carcass to give him an ecstatic embrace. "How can I help but fight when your life is in danger? Haven't I given you my secret name?"

"Yes," he said, "but I'm afraid you'll get hurt. So let me do all the killing. It's a business I understand."

That night by the fire, as they sat with half-closed eyes, Silver Hat saw Lady Grace in a different way— as a woman well fitted to be his mate. She was beautiful—but she was strong; her eyes were smiling—but they were fearless. She loved the rough life that had always been his, and, more than that, she loved him. It was not the love philter of base old Masawa that made her slender hand seek his. She loved him, she trusted him, she longed always to be near him, to share every hardship and danger. But would she, when they escaped?

For days now she had been his other self—a fairy creature, always at his side, always exercising strange wiles that made his heart leap and stop. But, out of their narrow valley, the world would intervene. There was her father, Lord Benedict, with his calm assumption that his daughter would obey him in everything, and stern-faced Major Doyle, waiting to question his scout, impatient at any delay. But what reason could he give for not making a signal fire—for putting it off day by day? Only his fear of the cattle thieves below, and they could not reach him now.

When the freezing hands of winter locked the waters at their source, then a boat, a man, a horse might conceivably stem the current that swept so irresistibly on. But now the stormy floods of midsummer were upon them and the river was running wild. From the shelter of their cabin they could hear roar after roar, as sand riffled the smooth waves of the rapids that led down to the point. It was time the signal fire was set.

"What are you thinking of, dear Silver Hat," she asked at last, "that makes you glare and frown? Are you fighting your battle with the lion all over again, as our hounds do at home by the fire?"

"No," he answered, "I am thinking of Major Doyle when he asks me about our signal fire. The last thing I told the scouts was to look out for my smoke. But we have been here four days and I haven't made a signal . . . I don't know what has come over me."

"It is the cattlemen below that you are afraid of. And, really, when one thinks how helpless we would be if by chance they should prove evil-minded . . ."

"But tell me this," he broke in, "how can they come up that river? Or down it, either, for that matter? I expect they're hard men . . . a bunch of cow thieves probably. But we're safe . . . they can't get to us."

"Then how can Desteen, and your scouts?"

"They can come over the mesa and look down from the cliffs. And if their ropes won't reach us, they can go back to the fort and bring out a hundred men."

"Yes . . . and what then?" She smiled. "Can any man scale those walls?"

"I doubt it," he replied. "I'd hate to try myself."

"And I," she spoke up, "would never consent to try. It's much safer to remain where we are."

"But, listen," he protested, "what are people going to say if they find us just living here . . . not even trying to escape?"

"They will say, if they know, that we have been very, very happy. Has it been only four days, Silver Hat?"

"Four days," he repeated, "and I haven't made a smoke. And me a government scout."

"They'll find us," she observed, sighing resignedly. "And then all this will come to an end."

She waved her hand at the fireplace, at him, at their two beds side by side, and Silver Hat nodded assent.

"But what days," she went on dreamily. "Are you so anxious to have it over? How pleasant it will be, now the lion is gone, to explore all the chasms and caves . . . to seek out old cliff dwellings, to bathe in the clear pool, to lie among the ferns to dry. Why is it, Silver Hat, that we always destroy our happiness by wondering what people will say? Even here, where there is no one to observe us?"

"It's because," he returned, "you've got a father outside there . . . and I'm a government scout. You're reported lost, maybe dead, to Washington and the British Embassy. How will it look, if I stay here, month by month, instead of trying to find some way out?"

"But do you know what will happen when we do

escape? I will be carried away bodily, bundled out of
the country . . . we will never see each other again.
Then why bother our heads about Washington and
the British Embassy and all the outside world that I
hate? Why not rest here a while in our hidden cañon
and try to realize what life really means? We can go
out every day, gathering seeds and chipmunk corn,
and, when the cows come in, we can catch their little
calves and make the mothers give us milk. It is a life
I have always dreamed of, even back in old England
where your least act is laid down from birth. And
then you can tan calfskin and provide me with
sinews to sew you a buckskin shirt. Everything will
be so free and happy with only you to think of, Silver Hat. And tomorrow we can go into the great valley beyond the bend and look for some passageway
out. But the moment you light that signal fire all our
dream life will come to an end."

She gazed across at him with half-veiled eyes that
seemed to read his inmost thoughts, and Silver Hat
bowed his head. He had saved her from the Hopis—
was that not enough for his $100 a month? And who
was her father that he should consider him before
this smiling, adorable Lady Grace who had given
him her secret name? What was a week, a month in
the long lifetime to come when he might never see
her more? He smiled back soberly, and with a
bound she was upon him, twining her arms about
his neck.

"Dear Silver Hat," she cried, kissing him joyously
on both cheeks. "And to think I should have this
respite . . . with you . . . when all the world seemed
flat and stale. Perhaps, if they do not come, we may
find the courage to bolt . . . to chuck it all and begin

life anew. But now every day shall be lived like our last . . . something to cling to, to treasure, without fear for the future or regrets. And every night I shall live it over in my dreams."

She rose up tremulously, and, as his blue eyes met hers, some message passed between them. It was a promise, a prophecy, and, as the days went by, the storms and turmoil ceased. A month passed and their supply of flour gave out, but in its place they had sacks of chipmunk corn that could be ground up into meal. From the huge nests of the pack rats they ravished stores of acorns, leaching out the bitter taste and making Indian bread, gathering bear grass seeds along the slopes. They had fresh meat from the yearlings that Silver Hat killed for their hides, and milk from a gentle old cow, but always, as they worked, he watched the towering cliffs—and the river, going down and down. Then one morning just at dawn he saw a smoke, heaven high, rising straight up from the highest crag, and, when Lady Grace beheld it, she wept.

CHAPTER TWENTY-FIVE

Pin-high on the distant cliff where the smoke signal rose, a slender form stood out, holding up a huge hat, and Silver Hat touched off his pyre. It was Jani, his Indian brother, and the sombrero was his own silver hat. They had found him at last and now in ascending puffs the smoke talk was going on.

"Come to us!" they said, and, without waiting for breakfast, Silver Hat and Grace ran across the valley. They could look up and see Jani and the other Navajos dangling a long rope over the rim, but it stopped midway down the first solid stratum and at last they drew it back. Then, terrace by terrace, Jani came down a long channel that flood waters had broken in the wall, but on the face of that mighty cliff he appeared like a fly and his rope like a spider's web.

"We go back!" he shouted, waving his hand to the east. "Go back and bring soldiers!"

"Tell them to come up the river . . . in boats!" answered Silver Hat, and at last Jani seemed to understand. He waved his hat again and disappeared from sight, leaving them standing in their sinkhole, alone. They hurried back to the cabin and their belated breakfast, and then in a fever of expectation they went out to the wide bench to wait. So lofty was the cliff, so confusing its echoes, that their words had passed back and forth faintly, but now that the scouts had discovered their hiding place, their rescue was but a matter of days.

Already they could feel distant eyes upon them, staring down from the heights through powerful field glasses, watching every move they made. But although they waited all day, no one appeared along the rim, and at sundown they went in by the fire.

"How futile it all seems," sighed Lady Grace. "And how silly we have been, sitting out there all day, when we might have been up at the spring. But now that they have found us, the soldiers will soon come. And *Pater* . . . and Major Doyle."

She sighed again and Silver Hat nodded grimly.

"Yes," he said, "and I'll need a few days to think up what to say . . . to the major."

"You can tell him," she answered, "that you were afraid to make signals on account of the cattle thieves below."

"I'll tell him nothing," responded Silver Hat, "and then hit the trail. That's the best way to do, when you're wrong."

"Why, Silver Hat," she exclaimed, "in what way are you wrong?"

"I don't know." He shrugged. "But the major will tell you. He's been hunting this country for a month."

"No. I think it was just Jani and that little band of scouts. How they jumped and danced when you waved your hand, and they heard your voice again!"

"It was Jani," he agreed. "He told me he would never give up. Now they're back to their horses and riding for the fort. I wonder if your father is still there."

"Why, of course!" she cried. "What a question to ask! But poor *Pater* . . . how he has suffered. I'm his only child . . . the last of the Benedicts. He wouldn't dare to return alone."

"And I reckon," he hinted darkly, "there are others, back in England, who will be glad to see you again."

"Oh, yes," she responded, avoiding his eyes, "I dare say I have given them quite a fright. Even to start for America was terrible enough. But to be lost in the mountains . . . to be taken captive by the Indians. Please let's talk of something else."

"All right," he agreed. "And you'd better say nothing about . . . well, all that."

He waved his hand toward the north and Lady Grace flushed and turned pale.

"And will *you* say nothing, too?" she asked at last. "It is very kind of you, Silver Hat."

"That's all right," he said. "I don't like to think about it myself. But, of course, I'll have to report to Major Doyle that Harold Polinuivah is dead."

"Very well." She nodded, and, rising up quickly, she put their supper over the fire. They ate in silence, each haunted by uneasy thoughts, but that evening, as they sat watching the flames, she gazed across at him wistfully.

"How nice you look," she said, "in your new calf-skin hunting shirt, and the buckskin leggings we made. Everything was going so well . . . we could have lived here all winter . . . but now the scouts have come. I wonder how they found us."

"Followed the cliffs down, I reckon," he answered. "Or maybe the Hopis told Jani. But what I'm wondering is whether those cow thieves happened to see our smoke this morning."

He rose up and threw down the heavy bar that fastened their door at night and Lady Grace's eyes grew big.

"Don't you know," she exclaimed, "I have felt all day as if somebody was watching . . . was coming! And yet, how could they come? There is no way but the river, and it has been so high."

"There's a storm up above," he said. "You can hear the rapids roar. But what are we going to say if these men do come up here, and ask who we are . . . and so on?"

"Why, tell them we were lost . . . that we came down the river and were thrown ashore at this place. Surely no one could blame us for killing a few cattle. And, of course, we will pay them well."

"Yes, but that isn't the point . . . these cattle are stolen. I know it by the brands. And if we get out alive, we're liable to tell about these cows. That's what I've got on my mind."

"You don't mean," she cried, aghast, "that they might kill us, Silver Hat, in order to conceal their guilt?"

"They might," he admitted. "It depends on who they are. This is a hard country, down below."

"Then I must go out to meet them," she decided, her eyes alight. "And when they see me, they'll be so surprised . . ."

"No, you run away and hide," he advised.

"But, Silver Hat," she reasoned, "I'm only a woman. They will know I wouldn't steal their cows. And I'll smile and be nice to them and tell them who I am. . . ."

"No, you run away and hide," he repeated. "I want to talk to them first."

"But they might shoot you," she protested. "When they saw you alone. Oh, I wonder if it could be that Crying Man that Harold Polinuivah spoke about."

"Harold," he repeated, dumbfounded. "Did he tell you about Crying Man?"

"Yes, he said there was an outlaw who lived at the ferry and stole horses and sheep from the Indians. Then he sold them to the Mormons and stole some of their horses to sell back to the Indians. Have you known about him all the time?"

"Well . . . yes," he acknowledged. "That's why I put out the fire that first time we made a smoke. But after thinking it over, I decided it was safer to signal while the river was high."

"And is he such a bad man?" she asked breathlessly. "Do you really consider him dangerous?"

"He's treacherous," he said. "That's the name he has . . . and, of course, I haven't got a gun. Did Harold ever tell you what he looked like?"

"No-o. But he did say he laughed a great deal. And, oh, I remember, he said . . . when he killed people . . . he cried."

"How do you mean?" he inquired with a frown.

"Why, he has rheumy eyes . . . the tears flow down his cheeks . . . but he isn't weeping at all. In fact, Harold said he laughed."

"My . . . God," breathed Silver Hat, and then he sat, silent. "Well, we'll know him," he said at last.

"Do you think he saw the smoke?" she inquired in a hushed voice. "Do you really expect him to come?"

"He couldn't help seeing it," he burst out. "Unless he lives down in the canon. But no man on earth can come up that river the way it's roaring tonight."

"But you do expect him, Silver Hat?"

"I've got a hunch," he said. "That's all. I'm nervous as a witch."

"And if he does come . . . what can we do? I don't want to run away."

"Well, hide in the cabin . . . keep yourself out of sight. I believe I can handle him alone."

"You mean you can reason with him, Silver Hat?"

"Yes," he said at last. "I want to get close to him. The trouble is I haven't got a gun."

"But if I should hear him speak threateningly . . . may I come out then? Something tells me that that would save you."

"It might," he admitted. "But what about you?"

"Oh, I'll be all right." She smiled. "I have heard so much about the chivalry of Western men . . . I'm sure a woman would be safe."

"Well . . . maybe," he said. "But what will we tell him if he asks, point-blank, who you are?"

"Why, tell him I am Lady Grace Benedict, the woman who was stolen at the Snake Dance."

"No, I don't mean that," he went on patiently. "We've been living here together a month, and to a man like him that probably means only one thing. And if he ever thinks you're that kind of a woman . . ."

"Why, Silver Hat!" she cried, starting back, and he heaved a great sigh.

"I'm sorry," he said, "but that's the way it is."

"Then I'll tell him we're married!" she declared.

"All right," he agreed. "I just wanted you to say so. We've struck a hard country, I'm afraid."

CHAPTER TWENTY-SIX

All night Silver Hat could hear Lady Grace turn and toss, but, although his eyes and ears were open, he lay still in his bed of straw, and at dawn he stepped out the door. Some of the wildest of the cattle, still drinking at night, were drifting away from the spring, but he could tell by their actions that no enemy was near—it was an obsession, a trick of the mind. There was no one in their valley but Lady Grace and himself, and the river was still running high. Yet, when the sun came up, each of them moved by the same impulse, they went out on the bench to watch.

"How silly," she said, smiling wanly, "for both of us to sit here all day. Yet so we did yesterday, and so we will do today. We might at least take turns."

"You go," he suggested, but she shook her head and moved closer.

"I want to be near you." She sighed. "But no one can come today. And if they did come, you would be better off without me. I am sorry I'm always in the way."

"I talked too much, last night," he confessed. "It's something that has been on my mind."

"All the time, Silver Hat? Ever since we came here? Then why didn't you mention it before?"

"It would only spoil your happiness," he answered, "without doing me any good. But now it's over, anyway. We're going to sit right here till a boat comes up that cañon, so we might as well talk straight out."

"Then I want to ask you," she began, "what you really intend to do. Why couldn't we both hide until they go away, instead of staying right here to meet them?"

"We can't hide," he said. "We're bottled up in this cañon. It wouldn't take an hour to roust us out of the rocks . . . and then what would we do? No, the thing is to stand pat and show we're on the square. Then if we have to . . . fight it out."

"I thought so." She nodded. "You intend to fight them alone."

"Well, why not?" he challenged. "That's my business . . . fighting. And if I ever get him up within reach of my hand, I can talk to him man to man."

"But there might be several," she objected. "And surely I can be of some help."

"Get me one of their guns," he said earnestly. "That's all I ask . . . one gun."

He fell into a silence, gazing with fixed eyes down the cañon, and at last she went into the house, but, as the afternoon sun swung low and nothing happened, she came out and sat beside him.

"It is too late now," she said. "They will not come today. And tomorrow, if they hurry, the soldiers will arrive. Wouldn't you like to have me watch a while?"

"Nope," he answered, still gloomily intent, and she glanced down the cañon with a sigh. Against the black point, the last of yesterday's flood was throwing up waves of gray spray, while up the mysterious gorge there came the rumble of distant rapids, the booming echo from some cave. But as she gazed, around the point a dark object appeared, and she clutched at Silver Hat's hand. It was a boat, barely moving against the rush of the current, but battling stubbornly on, and, as it rose on a wave, they saw a huge man, lashing back and forth with his oars.

"We'd better go inside," suggested Silver Hat quietly, and from the window they stared out in silence.

The man had passed the dangerous turn and now, bending low, was toiling up through the rapids. They caught the bristle of brick-red hair, the play of bulging muscles, as he shot into the big eddy below. Then for the first time he turned and they saw his bold face, set like iron from fighting the stream. For a moment he gazed, bowed once more to the oars, and still, standing breathless, they watched. With swift, deep strokes that showed no sign of weariness he glided toward them through the dimpling eddies, and then, striking the landing, he leaped nimbly overboard and dragged his skiff up on the shore.

"Is it Crying Man?" whispered Grace as the stranger stood erect, and Silver Hat hesitated before he spoke. The man was big, red-faced, virile, with protruding eyes that showed the whites, but every line of his countenance was grim.

"I don't think so," he answered, still watching, and suddenly the man started back. He glanced quickly to right and left as if something had alarmed him, then reached down and buckled on a gun belt and snatched a long rifle from the stern. It was an old-fashioned, single-shot needle-gun, and he stopped to shove a cartridge into the chamber.

"He lives here," whispered Silver Hat, "and he's seen something wrong. But let him come up close."

"But it isn't Crying Man, is it?" she insisted hopefully. "There aren't any tears on his cheeks."

"No, and he never laughed in his life," replied Silver Hat with conviction.

"Then let me go out first," she pleaded. "He's coming up, ready to shoot."

With stealthy steps, still looking to right and left, his rifle held to the front, the burly newcomer strode silently up the path, until, seeing tracks, he stopped. For a moment he stood, staring—then with eyes suddenly afire he advanced toward the cabin door. Lady Grace glanced up at Silver Hat and stepped out, smiling sweetly, but Silver Hat was close behind her. There had been no time for planning, and at sight of a white woman the big man stood frozen in his tracks.

"How do you do," she greeted. But he seemed not to hear her—and all the time his eyes were on Silver Hat.

"What are you doing here?" he yapped out fiercely. "Killing my cattle . . . eating up my grub!"

"We were shipwrecked up the cañon," interposed

Lady Grace, "and barely escaped with our lives. But we shall be very glad to pay you for everything, and thank you for its use besides."

He paused and lowered his gun, although the hammer remained cocked, and looked from her to Silver Hat. Then, seeing him unarmed, he turned to Lady Grace and his harsh voice was rougher than before.

"Oh, you will, hey?" he sneered. "Well, what will you pay me with? Did you bring your money ashore?"

"No, we saved nothing," she admitted. "But my father is very wealthy, and will be able to compensate you handsomely."

"Yes? And who is your father?" he asked.

"Horace, Lord Earl of Benedict. He is staying with Major Doyle at Fort Defiance."

"You don't say," he jeered, looking her over appraisingly. "A regular English lord, eh? And who is this big lad who has been so busy butchering my beef? By the gods, there are hides everywhere! You've killed half my herd. A thousand dollars wouldn't half pay for them."

He peered past her into the cabin, fingering his rifle lock nervously, but Lady Grace met his glance bravely.

"We will pay you well," she repeated. "This is my husband, Milton Buckmaster."

"Oh . . . Buckmaster," he said. "Seems to me I've heard that name. Where are you from, Buckmaster? Step out here."

He beckoned sternly with his rifle barrel and Silver Hat stepped out, although he was looking down the muzzle of the gun.

"I'm from Fort Defiance," he answered. "A government scout under Major Doyle. As for the cattle I've killed, I'll pay you back, two for one, if you'll take us out in your boat."

"Fair enough," returned the big man bluffly, "but my boat will only hold two. So I'll take the lady first."

He bowed sardonically to Lady Grace and suddenly her face went pale.

"Oh, no," she protested, coming up beside Silver Hat. "I don't wish to be separated from my husband."

"Your . . . husband." The big man leered, bursting out into a roar of laughter. "Don't try to tell me that. He's no more married than I am, and I ain't married at all. But still, with a good-looking girl like you, I'd be willing to take the name."

"Sir!" she cried, stepping back and flushing angrily, and the outlaw laughed again. As he laughed, suddenly the tears began to course down his cheeks. It was Crying Man, who laughed when he killed men. She stepped behind Silver Hat and gasped.

"And so you're Buckmaster," he went on, still chuckling malevolently. "I know you . . . know all about you . . . only they call you Silver Hat. Well, I'm busy right now . . . like to have a few words with the lady. You just walk up the valley . . . and don't you look back or I'll break you of stealing cows, permanent!"

He tapped his gun with the heel of his hand, and Silver Hat stood looking him in the eye. But before he could speak, Lady Grace stepped forward, smiling graciously.

"You may speak to me now," she said.

"Hah, hah, hah . . . I like that!" he roared. "You're

a good one . . . I like your style. And since that daddy of yours has gone back to England, I feel right free to speak my piece. You're supposed to be dead, so you'll never be missed . . . how'd you like to be my wife? Stay here, you understand, where nothing will disturb us. I'll bring you up lots of grub."

"Oh, no," she answered, blushing furiously. "I couldn't think of that. And please make no mistake. We have nothing, of course, having floated down the river on logs. But since you speak of my father, you have doubtless heard of Lady Grace, who was abducted by the Hopis at the Snake Dance. I was saved from their hands by Silver Hat, but we were afraid to venture farther down the river. So please treat us respectfully and take us to the fort, where my father will pay you any price."

"That's a fact," put in Silver Hat, edging closer. "He offered me her weight in gold if I would bring her back, unharmed."

"Oho!" Crying Man laughed, prodding playfully at him with the gun barrel. "So that's how the matter lies. He offered you the money but you took the lady . . . you preferred the gal to the gold! Well, I'm just as game a sport as you are . . . and, since we both can't have her . . ."

He whipped out his pistol, left handed, and with a swift single movement jabbed it against Silver Hat's side—and pulled. Silver Hat felt the savage jolt of the muzzle and caught his breath, expecting death. But instead of a flaming blast the pistol gave off a muffled *clank*. It had snapped—the cap had missed fire.

With all his strength Silver Hat struck out wildly, and, as he leaped upon his man, Lady Grace snatched the pistol and wrested it from Crying Man's grasp. The two men went down, fighting and choking, rolling over and over while each with his bare hands tried to do the other to death. But as he came up on top, Silver Hat reached back for his knife and stabbed him in the shoulder. Crying Man jumped at the bite of steel and with a terrible cry caught the hand before it fell again. Then in a paroxysm of fear he threw Silver Hat aside and went loping away up the cañon. Silver Hat picked up the long rifle and, aiming from one knee, drew a bead on Crying Man's back, but before he could shoot, Lady Grace joggled the gun, then pushed it quickly aside.

"Don't shoot him!" she cried, and, while he glared up angrily, the broad back disappeared among the rocks.

CHAPTER TWENTY-SEVEN

For the first time in their life together, Lady Grace saw Silver Hat fighting mad. His eyes gleamed wickedly as he sprang to his feet, marking down his enemy's flight while he pushed her furiously away.

"Keep your hands off that gun!" he ordered. "Do you want that wild hyena running loose?"

"But you wouldn't shoot a man in the back!" she cried.

"Shoot him anywhere," he answered, "before he shoots me."

"But he's unarmed, Silver Hat. I have his pistol."

"Yes, and what about tonight, when I can't see to kill him? Do you want him breaking in our door? We're shut up together in this cañon. One or the other must die."

"Oh, but, Silver Hat," she implored as he started up the cañon, "don't follow him and shoot him like a dog. He's a terrible creature, I know, but that would be plain murder."

"Well, what do you call it when he rams a pistol

into my ribs . . . and pulls the trigger? A man like
that deserves no mercy, and he'll get none from me.
Besides, I've got you to think of."

He ran off up the cañon, but she followed along
behind him.

"I'll tell you," she called, "let's take his boat and
leave him here! That would be a fitting punishment
for his treachery. And just think, Silver Hat . . . we can
escape now! We can row down the river and . . ."

"I never rowed a boat in my life," he flung back
over his shoulder.

"Oh, but I have," she pleaded. "Back home, on the
river. . . ."

He paused, irresolute, scanning the side of the
cañon with its huge, broken boulders behind which
Crying Man was hiding, until at last, reluctantly, he
yielded.

"But what good will it do," he urged, "if we do
float down the river? Getting out of this cañon is only
a starter . . . it's over a hundred miles to the fort."

"But I'm sure we can cover it," she urged. "And
the soldiers will be coming soon. We can take that
big canteen and a sack of dried meat and travel day
and night."

"Well, we've got to go now," he grumbled. "I
wouldn't spend a night in this cañon . . ."

"Oh . . . no!" she cried in a panic. "With that terrible creature at the door? I'm so sorry, Silver Hat, that
I struck up your gun. You know best, I know, and I'll
promise you faithfully never to interfere with your
aim again. Oh, how I felt when I saw him trying to
kill you. I was frightened . . . I couldn't move . . . and
then his pistol missed fire. But see, *we* have it now."

She displayed the heavy six-shooter that she had

wrenched from his grasp and Silver Hat laid hold of it lovingly.

"Good for you," he said, thrusting it into his waistband. "We got his guns, anyhow."

"Yes, I remembered what you said, and the moment he drew his pistol I snatched it with both hands."

"That's the stuff." He nodded. "And I gave him a knife jab that he won't forget in a hurry. The only trouble is, he got away with his cartridge belt . . . so this rifle will only shoot once."

"But we don't need to shoot at all," she protested. "Let's pack up our food and start immediately, before something terrible happens."

"Well, if anything terrible happens," he said, "it will happen to him. But when we come out at Mormon Ferry, we will have his whole gang on our hands."

"Oh, Silver Hat!" she cried, clutching his hand. "Will they all be like him . . . so rough and brutal?"

"I reckon so," he answered. "I wouldn't take a chance with them . . . with you along. It would be the same thing all over again."

"Then we must row right past them," she decided resolutely. "And if they threaten us again . . . I hope you kill them."

"I'll do that," he responded, "with all the pleasure in life. They're just like wild animals to me."

He stepped out into the open, the rifle at the ready, and, when Grace came hurrying out with the food and a canteen, he was looking up the cañon intently.

"He heard us," he said. "He knows what we're up to. I saw him sneaking down through the rocks."

"Then, if he comes," she spoke up clearly, "I want

you to kill him." And, tugging at his arm, she led him away. But down at the skiff, while Lady Grace was stowing her bundles, Silver Hat saw a head pop up over a rock. His finger was pressing the trigger before Crying Man saw him—and then, like a flash, he was gone.

"Now, Silver Hat," spoke up Lady Grace gently as he turned away from his search, "we must prepare for a spill, of course. So take off your hunting shirt and moccasins and tie your hair up with this."

She handed him a thong of buckskin, and, while he stood, wild-eyed, staring out at the river, she stripped off her own moccasins and tunic. Then she bound up her yellow hair and stepped forth, smiling radiantly.

"If he can row up it, I can row down," she said. "And yet, one never knows. So you sit in the stern, and, if the boat goes over, just catch the bottom and hold on."

He gazed back up the cañon, seeking hopefully for Crying Man, his rifle still ready to shoot. Then reluctantly he laid it down and stripped for the swim, although his eyes had a stony stare.

"Are you afraid?" she asked, standing now beside him, her warm body pressed against his. "I know how it is . . . you fear the water. But I will take care of you, Silver Hat. If we overturn in the rapids, I will swim beside you and support you till we reach the boat. Only trust me, Silver Hat, as I trust you on land. Shall we kiss good-bye again?"

She looked up at him, smiling, her lips parted for the kiss, and the frozen fear in his breast gave way. He held her closely in a long, parting embrace, and stepped down into the boat. She shoved it away from the shore and leaped nimbly in, and the great river bore them away.

After weeks of waiting, of watching flood after flood as it rushed, roaring, around the black point, Lady Grace and Silver Hat found themselves drawn at last into the swirl of this unknown maelstrom. Day after day they had come down to the landing and watched the surge of the stream, hearing the roar of the sand as it passed through the rapids, gazing with awe into the sucking hole of the whirlpool. But neither had had the courage to venture forth again until necessity drove them on. Only the vision of Crying Man, creeping in like a wild animal, cast them off from their beloved shore.

Grace laid hold of the oars and feathered them skillfully as she leaned forward for her first long stroke, and, as the boat darted ahead, she looked over her shoulder at the echoing chasm below. The sharply cleft black walls that resounded so thunderously to the roar of waters below rose higher and higher till they cut off the sky except for a vivid strip of blue. The air that drew up the cañon was damp with the reek of mud, slapped up against the slimy cliffs, and, as they shot down the rapids, the boat tossed like a cork, riding precariously on top of the waves. Then in a splash of muddy spray, they whipped around the point and Silver Hat gripped his seat.

Before them like a millrace the great river swept on, crowded closely between polished walls, but, half turning on the thwart, Lady Grace sat balanced, dipping lightly as she kept in midstream. A boiling wave loomed before her and she avoided the hidden rock, picking her way in and out, just on the edge of the rough water, riding high as they passed over some roll. Silver Hat's eyes were bleak as a huge backwash buffeted them and they were snatched around another point, but always before him he beheld her graceful form and in her eyes a wild, glad smile. With the boat beneath her and the ash oars in her hands, she rode the rapids like a conqueror until they glided out into still flowing water.

"Isn't it wonderful!" she cried, gazing up at the sunlit walls where trailing ferns occasionally clung. "Like hanging gardens . . . and look at the flowers! I wish it would last forever!"

She rested on her oars, floating peacefully along beneath long slopes that swept up to the sky, then, as a roar sounded ahead, she bent to her oars while she nodded with a mischievous smile.

"A man isn't everything," she observed oracularly. "Now see what a woman can do!"

An undulating stretch of water appeared before them, and she rode it deftly, still looking beyond, and, as a tumult arose, she headed straight into it, rising high as she took the first wave. Then, bobbing and turning, she shot the rapids safely and glided into the eddy below.

"Oh, I love it," she sighed. "You must learn water, Silver Hat. With a good boat and a stout pair of blades you can laugh at old Tayholtsdi."

Her eyes danced with joy as with slow, steady strokes she rowed between the overhanging walls, and, as he felt the skiff cut the water, the cold fear left Silver Hat's narrowed eyes. He let go of the thwart, but when she spoke of Tayholtsodi, he scowled and shook his head.

"You be careful," he warned. "And don't talk about that water god. Just wait till we get ashore."

"You're nothing but a Navajo," she taunted, "but Britannia rules the waves. Now say your prayers . . . I can hear another roar. I just love to shoot these rapids."

Silver Hat touched his lips and the top of his head, tossing his hand up to heaven as if it bore corn pollen for all the Navajo gods, but, as they whipped around a point, they darted out into hot sunshine and the river walls opened before them. Then, huge and unsightly on the Utah side of the stream, a ferryboat loomed up ominously. A cable hung above it, and down on the shore a bearded man stood at gaze.

"Pull over," said Silver Hat, jerking his thumb to the left. "We've come to Mormon Ferry."

CHAPTER TWENTY-EIGHT

The water at Mormon Ferry was smooth and still, barely rippled by dimpling swirls, but below the first point the cañon began again, and from its mouth they could hear a deep roar. Lady Grace rowed steadily; Silver Hat picked up his pistol and laid his rifle across his knees, and still, as if frozen, the bearded man at the ferry stood staring up the river. Not an hour before big Ben Ammon had rowed away in his boat. Now it came back with *two* passengers—and the one at the oars was a woman, stripped to the waist.

She rowed evenly, smoothly, her white back gleaming as it caught the rays of the sun, while in the stern a tall man took his ease, waving his hand toward the opposite shore. For a full minute's time the outlaw stood at gaze, but, as the boat drew near and he could make out their features, he barked a sudden challenge.

"Hey! Come in hyer! Where's Ben?" he shouted, and from the door of a log cabin against the cliff two men thrust out their heads.

"Up the cañon," Silver Hat answered briefly, and Lady Grace swung toward the opposite shore.

"But what are you doing with his boat?" he yelled back. "Come over hyer! What's the matter with you?"

"We borrowed it," returned Silver Hat, "to come here."

Lady Grace stepped out and, snatching up her clothes, made a dash for a grove of cottonwoods, but Silver Hat, picking up his rifle, stood facing them, ready to shoot.

"Hey! Who are you?" the bearded ferryman called.

"Silver Hat . . . government scout! You can charge this to Uncle Sam."

"Yes, but who's that woman?" bawled the ferryman impatiently, and the two men above came running down.

"Never mind," responded Silver Hat. "I'll leave your boat here." And he pulled it up on the shore.

Across the wide waters Silver Hat could hear every word as the three men talked together.

"You bring back that skiff!" one of them ordered. "What the devil are you trying to do?"

"I'm minding my own business," said Silver Hat, sitting down to put on his moccasins. But as he rose to pull on his hunting shirt, there came a shout from the cañon's mouth. Then, floating around the bend on a bobbing log, he beheld the red head of Crying Man.

"Stop that bastard!" he howled, rousing the echoes of the high cliffs with his curses. "I say stop him . . . he stole my boat! But don't hurt the woman! Be careful now!"

Silver Hat raised the rifle as one of the men drew

a pistol, and no one fired a shot. They huddled together, unable to understand why their chief should be floating on a log.

"Shoot!" he raged. "Kill the murdering bastard! He stabbed me in the back and took my boat! Don't you let him git away!"

He rose up on his log to shout louder, but when Silver Hat brought the long rifle to his shoulder, he ducked down out of sight.

"Git yore rifles!" he ordered angrily, "before the damned whelp finishes me! But don't hit the woman, boys! She's worth her weight in gold!"

"Silver Hat!" cried Lady Grace. "Please come behind the trees!" At the flash of a rifle barrel from the door of the cabin, he took shelter among the cottonwoods. Then a bullet came slashing its way through the branches, and they both dropped down out of sight. There was a volley of shots, the leaves fell in showers as the slugs passed over their heads, and as suddenly the shooting stopped. From behind his big log, Crying Man was shouting orders and Silver Hat rose up to listen.

"Stop that shooting!" he bellowed again. "And don't hit the woman . . . she's mine! Go on down to the pasture and bring up the horses! They cain't git away from us now!"

"Oh, dear," lamented Lady Grace. "Are they going to come across and catch us?"

"Not while I'm here with this rifle," responded Silver Hat. "I'll kill the first man that starts."

"We were doing so nicely," she sighed. "And then *he* had to come."

"I should have killed him when I could," said Silver Hat. "But it's you they're after now."

"For my weight in gold?" she quavered. "Did *Pater* really make you that offer? Then why didn't you tell me before?"

"What's the difference?" he grumbled. "I wouldn't accept the money. But I thought Crying Man might consider it."

"What a brute he is!" she exclaimed. "I wish you had killed him now. But I'd always heard, Silver Hat, that Western men were so chivalrous toward women!"

"Good men," he corrected. "Toward good women. But we gave him the wrong idea."

"Then what can we do?" she asked.

"Either stay and shoot it out," he said, "or make a run for the fort."

"Oh, let's run, then," she proposed. "We can travel all night. And perhaps the Navajos will meet us."

"They'll be up on the high mesa, going in toward our cañon. But if we light a big fire and make smoke talk . . ."

"I'll start one!" she cried, leaping up, and, while Silver Hat with his rifle watched the river, she gathered a great pile of sticks. Then, opening her bundle, she brought out a block of matches and set it in a blaze. The flames leaped up in a mighty roar as she threw on the bone-dry wood, and, when they were at their height, she broke off green branches and piled them on top of the fire.

Three men rode up on the opposite side as the signal smoke rose to the sky, but at sight of Silver Hat with his rifle ready to shoot they ducked back out of sight. There was no crossing the wide river, by boat or by horse, as long as he guarded the way, and, as evening approached, Silver Hat broke off a big limb and smothered down the smoke. Then he removed it quickly, sending up a huge puff, and laid it down again. High up into the still air the signals floated and the outlaws looked across uneasily.

"Hey!" hollered the ferryman, stepping out with his hand up, "what's the idee . . . setting that fire?"

"I'm signaling to the Navajos," answered Silver Hat, and the bearded outlaw laughed.

"This is Paiute country!" he whooped. "They ain't a Navvy for a hundred miles."

"You just wait," warned Silver Hat, "and I'll show you different. And the first man that starts across this river . . ."

"Never you mind!" bellowed Crying Man, stepping defiantly out the doorway. "We'll git you, my smart young lad! But if you give up that girl . . . ?"

Silver Hat whipped up his rifle and with a smothered oath Crying Man ducked back out of sight. Then behind the high cliff the sun died in a golden flame, and in the darkness the fugitives slipped away. Up over the narrow dug-way where Mormon ox-teams had broken a road, Lady Grace led the way, walking fast, while Silver Hat, behind, listened intently for their pursuers' hoof beats. But no one followed and far into the night they hurried on to the east.

A painted cliff rose on their left, barring them off from a straight course, throwing them constantly farther south, until at last just at dawn they rounded the last point and their home country opened up before them. Lady Grace sank down wearily. Silver Hat laid aside his gun, and, as the dim light illuminated the long trail behind, he searched it out with bloodshot eyes.

Traveling and resting by turns, pressed on by a great fear, they had covered nearly thirty miles, but now the pitiless rays of the sun would expose them to their enemies. He turned and looked to the east, where up a broken valley the road wound in and out among the cedars, but not a smoke, not a dust cloud rose to give him new hope. They were alone in that vast desert, and soon enough on their trail they would see the dust of pursuit.

"Here goes nothing," said Silver Hat, gathering an armful of brush. "We're out in the open ... they're sure to find us, anyway. I'm going to light a fire."

Rousing up from her apathy, Lady Grace nodded assent and laid on a few cedar sticks. Then the flames rose straight up, and Silver Hat piled on green tops until the smoke formed a pillar against the sky. The sun was rising in the east, where ridge on ridge of junipers barred the way to the Rio Bravo beyond. It was the Indians' hour for signaling, when every warrior's eye swept the horizon for some thin column of smoke, and, stripping off his hunting shirt, Silver Hat held it over the fire, then sent up a billowing puff. They mounted, puff by puff, until the wind from the high mesa seized the smoke and bent it to the south, and at last, far to the east on the rim of the cliff, an answering column shot up.

"We win," announced Silver Hat, "there's Jani!" And suddenly Lady Grace was in his arms.

"Oh, Silver Hat," she sobbed. "Have we escaped them at last? What cruel, heartless men, to chase us like wild animals ... to try to hold me for my weight in gold."

"We fooled them." Silver Hat laughed. "They were

afraid to cross the river . . . they're still watching that cottonwood fire. And before they can get here . . ." He paused, and she followed his eyes. From a cañon behind them four horsemen had suddenly appeared, galloping madly toward their smoke.

"Get down behind these rocks," directed Silver Hat, seizing his rifle. "I'll stand them off until the Navajos come. And you keep up the fire, so Jani can find us. That's Crying Man and his gang."

He piled boulder after boulder in a circle to form a rough barricade, while Lady Grace, hurrying out, gathered fresh armfuls of brush and heaped them on the dying fire. Then over a rise the spurring horsemen came racing, and Silver Hat cocked his gun. He lay silently waiting, his finger on the trigger, his foresight on the man in the lead; until suddenly with a *whang* the heavy rifle spoke and Crying Man pitched into the dirt. Silver Hat threw aside the gun and drew his long pistol, crouching down to await their charge, but at the fall of their leader the outlaws broke right and left, circling around to cut them off.

Behind their pile of rocks, Silver Hat and Grace lay closely together, watching the ridges for the first sign of a charge, while high up on the cliff a line of savage horsemen went galloping on into the west. It was Jani and his scouts, seeking a trail down the bluff. The steep wall cut them off, and, as Silver Hat crouched down, waiting, he felt the ground tremble beneath him. Then behind him he heard the thunder of approaching hoof beats and rose up to shoot it out. But in place of the outlaws he beheld a squad of soldiers, and in the lead rode Major Doyle himself.

"Well, damn me!" The major grinned, dropping

down off his horse. "If I didn't take you both for Indians! What's all this shooting ahead?"

Silver Hat turned, and down the trail he heard a sudden fusillade and the high-pitched Navajo war cry.

"That's Jani," he said, "and the outlaws that were after us. It's Crying Man's gang from Mormon Ferry."

"Were they trying to kill you?" barked the major, and in a flash he had mounted and was gone. But close upon his heels there came another squad of troopers and Lady Grace leaped up, waving.

"There's *Pater!*" she cried, and, as the soldiers swept past, Lord Benedict swung down from his horse.

"Why, dearest!" he exclaimed, rushing forward to meet her, and Silver Hat turned away.

It was all over—in a minute—the long quest and flight, the days when Lady Grace was always with him, and at a yell from down the trail he ran to meet Jani, riding up on his own blooded horse. They met in a wild embrace, Desteen hugged him eagerly, the Navajos crowded in to greet him, and then, suddenly grave, they advanced to meet Slender Woman and shake hands, one by one.

"*Ahalani!*" they shouted, and she smiled as she took their hands.

"*Ahalani,*" she responded, and old Desteen nodded benignly. She was learning the ways of the Dineh. Then Jani seized Silver Hat and lifted him up on his horse, which whinnied as it sensed its master, and with his big hat on his head and the Navajos galloping behind, Silver Hat rode back into camp.

CHAPTER TWENTY-NINE

Over the first wooded ridge from where Silver Hat had made his stand, they came to the soldiers' camp, and after a hasty breakfast he took shelter in a tent and slept till the sun was low. When he awoke, Lord Benedict was standing at the entrance, looking in with a deprecating smile.

"May I come in?" he asked, and Silver Hat grunted sleepily as he roused up and shook his head. Then, pouring out a basin of water, he washed the sweat from his eyes and looked up. His lordship, still waiting, cleared his throat and stepped in, and Silver Hat dropped back in his blankets.

"I wish to thank you again," began Lord Benedict affably, "for saving my daughter's life. Poor child, she is very grateful, and, before she fell asleep, she spoke warmly of your courage and devotion. But, of course, you understand that, no matter what your sentiments may be, this friendship with Lady Grace must end."

Silver Hat opened his tired eyes and regarded him a moment—and now his lordship's face was grim.

"Oh, sure," muttered Silver Hat, "I understand."

"Of course," went on Lord Benedict, "we shall never forget your gallant conduct, and we esteem you very highly as a man. But there is a fine, young English gentleman waiting anxiously for her return . . . Lionel George, Viscount Bramwell, Earl of Bramwell. So, of course, that ends it all."

"I reckon so," responded Silver Hat, rising up, and Lord Benedict surveyed him blankly.

"I suppose," he suggested, "my daughter has mentioned him? You have been some time together."

"Yes, she mentioned him," answered Silver Hat, feeling around under the blankets. "I wonder what happened to my six-shooter."

"Here it is," replied his lordship, turning it up with his riding boot. "That's a vicious-looking knife you carry."

"Yes, I need it in my business," returned Silver Hat. "And now, if you'll excuse me, I'll go over with the Indian scouts and see what they've got to eat."

"Oh, yes, yes . . . certainly. I know you must be hungry. But before we part, I am reminded of my promise . . . my daughter's weight in gold, you know."

"Her what?" demanded Silver Hat, waking up.

"Why, her ransom. The reward, for bringing her back unharmed. You must pardon my mentioning it, but we shall be starting for California the moment the poor child awakens."

"Oh, that's all right," returned Silver Hat, starting off.

Over at the Indian camp, he sat down with the Navajos and ate hugely from the common pot. Then he rose up, ignoring his lordship, who had followed, and spoke a few words to Jani.

"Ah, Mister Silver Hat," began Lord Benedict as he strode away, "may I have a few more words with you? About the reward now, there will be no splitting of hairs over her weight. I have brought our wagon along, containing the gold. And considering the service you have rendered, I am going to give you all of it."

"Well, she's worth it, all right," said Silver Hat at last, and his lordship's anxious face lit up.

"Oh, a thousand times over!" he cried. "I'm only sorry I can't give you more. Won't you come with me a moment . . . here's our wagon, right over here. I wish to show you a very ingenious device."

He hurried over to the yellow wagon that had borne them so far, and after a moment's hesitation Silver Hat followed with a cynical smile.

"Now, observe closely," warned Lord Benedict, touching a panel in the floor, and at a jab against a bolt in the side of the wagon the panel slid smoothly open. "There are your sovereigns," he announced dramatically, and in the dim light Silver Hat caught the gleam of gold.

The coins lay snugly stored in a hidden false bottom, some in bags tightly tied, others loosely displayed before his eyes.

"You accept, of course," spoke up a voice in his ear, and Silver Hat stared at the wealth before him.

"Oh, sure," he answered bluffly. "But don't say anything to her. She might not like it if she thought I took the money. So you just keep it until I come back for it . . . and tell her I said . . . good-bye."

Silver Hat turned on his heel, just as Jani rode up with his horse, and without a word he swung up into the saddle and clapped his silver hat on his head. Then he jogged off into the dusk, leaving Lord Benedict, goggle-eyed, gazing after him in frank amazement.

"My word!" he exclaimed. "He's a cool one, I must say. But after all, the boy is right. He sees the situation . . . and why have a scene? I call that quite topping . . . quite gentlemanly. And how fortunate for me that dear Grace is still asleep. I must go over and see how she is."

He peeped in through the tent flap and, finding her still sleeping, smiled indulgently and tiptoed away. When he returned, it was dark, and by the light of a candle, Grace was fluffing out her golden hair.

"Why, my dear," he protested as he entered, "have you forgotten the use of a comb? Here is your toilet case, right here, yet you are using your fingers, for all the world like a savage. I really think it is high time we were getting on to California, where we can take the railway to New York. You have had your fling, your great adventure to relate to your children and grandchildren, but all things must come to an end, and we have Lionel George to consider. Here is a letter from him that came during your absence. Would you like to read it now?"

He handed it over briskly and she regarded it silently.

"Where's Silver Hat?" she asked at last.

"Oh, off with the Navajos," he answered easily. "You have gowns, you know, in the wagon."

"Why, surely." She laughed. "But how do you like my tunic? We made it together at Lost Cañon."

"Very suitable, under the circumstances," he replied. "But . . . well, hardly becoming to your station, now that all that is left behind. So come out to the wagon, dearest, and put on your other clothes."

He led the way in his tight-fitting riding trousers and loosely belted outing coat, but, as Lady Grace stepped into her wagon boudoir, she started back and set down the candle.

"Why, Father," she exclaimed, "the panel is open! Look at the sovereigns! Have we been robbed?"

"Oh, no," he answered, hastily closing the false door. "They are all there, I am sure."

"But . . . then why did you leave it open?"

"Well, if you must know, my dear," he admitted, "I was giving them to Silver Hat, as a reward for bringing you back. It was a wonderful feat, and quite worth the money. . . ."

"And did he accept it?" she demanded breathlessly.

"Oh, yes. But quite coolly, without a word of thanks. I can't quite make him out."

"Why, Father!" she exclaimed, putting her hand to her cheek, and then she sank down on a seat.

"Ah, here's your letter," he reminded her. "From Lionel George, you know. The dear boy must be quite concerned over the reports of your abduction."

He passed the missive over and she accepted it listlessly.

"What did he say?" she asked at last.

"Why, how should I know?" He laughed. "Open the letter and read."

"No, I mean Silver Hat," she spoke up sharply. "Where is he? Has he gone?"

"Yes, dear. He rode off with Jani at dusk."

"Then what about the money?"

Lord Benedict stood staring, a perplexed frown on his brow.

"That is rather strange," he confessed. "But he told me to keep it until he came back for it . . . and to tell you he said good-bye."

"Good-bye," she repeated, starting up. "He's gone! Without a word!"

"Well, yes. We thought it was best."

"But, Father, you don't understand him. Silver Hat is never coming back for that gold. Did you mention Lionel?"

"I did take the liberty, now that all this must end. . . ."

"Where did he go?" she demanded, leaping out. Then, as her father began to speak, she saw Desteen in the camp of the Navajos, standing wrapped in his blanket by the fire.

"You have spoiled it all!" she burst out accusingly. "You know how I hate Lionel George. Now let me alone. I won't have you interfering." And she ran over to the Indians' camp.

"*Hahdee* . . . Sombrero Plato?" she asked, making signs, and the old man beamed on her benignly.

"*Hola,*" he said. "I don't know."

"Yes, you do," she answered. "You take your crystal . . . so . . . and look up at the stars . . . so. You tell me where he is."

For a moment, he stood looking at her, his grim face Sphinx-like. Then he nodded and held out his hand.

"*Besos,*" he said, ". . . money." And Lady Grace ran back to the wagon.

"There!" she panted, pouring out a handful of sovereigns. "I want you to do hand-shaking, too. You help me find Sombrero Plato."

"Good," he grunted. And while he went out into the silence, she traded the rest of her sovereigns for a horse.

CHAPTER THIRTY

Standing alone beneath the stars, Desteen held up his pointed crystal, which itself was a fallen star, and over its perfect point he gazed along at one blinking orb until it drew nearer and nearer. Then in a vision he saw Silver Hat, riding fast toward the east, and came back and stood by the fire.

"He is there," he said, pointing, and Lady Grace took his hand.

"You come," she commanded. "Help me find him."

For the space of a minute he gazed into her eager eyes as though reading her inmost thoughts.

"*Yáhehteh* . . . good," he answered, and swung up on his horse. Lady Grace reined in behind him, and, before her father could cry out, they had vanished into the night.

They were lost in the outer darkness, beneath the shadows of high cliffs, riding unseen trails into the east, and along the road below they could hear the pounding of hoofs as the soldiers took up the chase. But as if led by an unseen hand, Desteen loped on through the cedars while the stars rose higher in the heavens. Then they entered a wide gap through the broken hills and before them the ground sloped away. Hidden from view beneath the black canopy of night the Painted Desert lay below them, and Desteen made a fire.

He crouched down by it singing, pouring corn pollen down his fingers, making sacrifice to Tinlehi and the winds, and, as his hand began to tremble, he talked to it earnestly, pointing east, pointing north, pointing south. Then suddenly it struck down, and he rose up smiling.

"Sombrero Plato," he said, and pointed to the south.

"Oh, he's going to Mexico!" cried Lady Grace in dismay.

"*Sí* . . . Mexico," he nodded, mounting.

"Then hurry!" she ordered, and the old man whipped his horse until he came to another pass.

The Pleiades had swung past with Orion in close pursuit and the great Scorpion hung high in the east, but when Desteen made a fire and waved his blanket before it, another blazed up on the plain. He moved his blanket to one side and swung it quickly back again, sending winks of light out into the night, and from the distant fire there came answering winks until the old man turned back and smiled.

"Sombrero Plato," he said again, pointing down at the fire, and headed out into the desert.

They rode recklessly now, across wide sand flats and deep washes, until suddenly before his fire Silver Hat rose up and stood, waiting.

"Oh, Silver Hat!" she cried tremulously as he reached up to help her down, and, as he lifted her to the ground and felt her arms about his neck, he kissed her and held her closely.

"How could you leave me," she reproached, "without even saying good-bye? After all the long days we were together?"

"Your father said good-bye for you," he answered gravely. "But now he's likely to be losers."

"You mean . . . ?" she asked, and stopped.

"I'm thinking of stealing you," he said.

"They why did you run away?" she demanded.

"Well, to keep from stealing you." He laughed. "But now I can see I was wrong. What do I care for Lionel George, Viscount Bramwell, and all the rest of it?"

"Oh, Silver Hat," she cried, "did Father tell you about him? And was that why you went away? Then let's sit down by the fire . . . I wish to explain. But where is Desteen . . . and Jani?"

"They're gone," he said as he threw down a saddle blanket. "They're great to disappear when they know they're not wanted. So here we are . . . you and me . . . alone."

He sank down by the fire, and, after a startled glance around, Lady Grace sat down at his side. The great desert was still, while above them like diamond points a million stars gleamed in the sky.

"It's so beautiful," she sighed, reaching out for his hand. "Do you remember when I gave you my secret name? We were sitting out on the bench, waiting for the lion to be snared, and talking about life . . . and fate. And we spoke of how you fled, that other time . . . only something drew you back. But would I have given you that name, and kissed you the way I did, if I had intended to go back to Lionel? I crossed the Río Bravo to escape from all that. Death was nothing, if it came, compared to the living death of going back to England . . . and him. But what did Father say?"

"Never mind," he answered angrily. "He made it plain what he thought of me, trying to give me your weight in gold. I'm not even a man that you'd thank in a decent way . . . I'm just some damned outlaw with a vicious-looking knife that happened to save his daughter. So now, if I happen to steal you, I'll not worry much about him. Lionel George's loss will be my gain . . . how would you like to live like this all your life?"

He waved at the fire, the horses hobbled out, the morning star glowing in the east, and she laid her head against his breast.

"Very much," she said simply, "if you really want me, Silver Hat. But if you think I'm not the woman to share all your hardships . . ."

"Oh, you're the woman." He laughed. "You're a regular Navajo. I just wanted to see if you knew how to find me . . . and I gave you one last chance to escape."

"How do you think I found you?" she asked.

"You hired old Desteen to do a little hand-shaking. And, now you're here . . . you're mine."

He put his arm about her and held her closely, and, as he felt her heart beat against his breast, he leaned over, demanding a kiss. But she buried her face and said: "No."

"But why not?" he asked, his voice breaking. "Don't you think I'm on the square? Are you afraid to trust me now?"

"You must ask in a certain way," she said.

"What way?" he pleaded as he felt her arms about his neck, her warm breath against his cheek. But she turned her lips away.

"Silver Hat," she reproached, "have you forgotten my secret name, and all the sweet promises I made? I loved you so, when I whispered it in your ear. When you speak it, I shall be yours."

Then it came to him suddenly, the name never spoken in the long days they dwelt together in Lost Cañon.

"Dear Love," he repeated. "Please give me a kiss. Promise to stay here and be my wife."

"Yes, Silver Hat," she answered, and her eager lips met his. "Everything that I have is yours."

"Then give me another kiss," he said.

ABOUT THE AUTHOR

DANE COOLIDGE was born in Natick, Massachusetts. He moved early to northern California with his family and was graduated from Stanford University in 1898. In his summers he worked as a field collector and in 1896 was employed by the British Museum in this capacity in northern Mexico. Coolidge's background as a naturalist is a trademark in his Western fiction, along with his personal familiarity with the vast, isolated regions of the American West and its deserts—especially Death Valley. Coolidge married Mary Roberts, a feminist and a professor of sociology at Mills College, in 1906. In the summers, these two ventured among the Indian nations and together they co-authored non-fiction books about the Navajos and the Seris. *Hidden Water* (1910), Coolidge's first Western novel, marked the beginning of a career that saw many of his novels serialized in magazines prior to book publication. There is an extraordinary breadth in these novels from *Wunpost* (1920), set in Death Valley, to *Maverick Makers* (1931), a Texas Rangers story.

Many of his novels are concerned with prospecting and mining, from *Shadow Mountain* (1920) and *Lost Wagons* (1923), based on actual historical episodes in the mining history of Death Valley, to a fictional treatment of Colonel Bill Greene's discovery of the fabulous Capote copper mine in Mexico, a central theme in *Wolf's Candle* (1935) and *Rawhide Johnny* (1936). *The New York Times Book Review* commented on *Hell's Hip Pocket* (1939) that "no other man in the field today writes better Western tales than Dane Coolidge." Coolidge, who died in 1940, wrote with a definite grace and leisurely pace all but lost to the Western story after the Second World War, although Nelson C. Nye, an admirer of Coolidge, tried in his own fiction to capture this same ambiance. The attention to the land and accurate detail make a Dane Coolidge Western story rewarding to readers of any generation.

DANE COOLIDGE

THE WILD BUNCH

Abner Meadows is only trying to get out of the storm when he seeks shelter in the cave. One of the most notorious bandits of the West, Butch Brennan, just happens to be in the same cave...with the loot from his latest holdup. Meadows knows better than to accept Brennan's offer to join his gang, but he is still stuck with the robber's recognizable horse and a few gold pieces.

Back in town, the sheriff raises a posse, and when they catch Meadows on Brennan's horse and then find his double eagles, they're convinced they've got their man. But Meadows will do anything to prove his innocence, including risking his life to track down the wild bunch that framed him.

Dorchester Publishing Co., Inc.
P.O. Box 6640 ___5374-8
Wayne, PA 19087-8640 $4.99 US/$6.99 CAN

Please add $2.50 for shipping and handling for the first book and $.75 for each additional book. NY and PA residents, add appropriate sales tax. No cash, stamps, or CODs. Canadian orders require an extra $2.00 for shipping and handling and must be paid in U.S. dollars. Prices and availability subject to change. **Payment must accompany all orders.**

Name: _____

Address: _____

City: _____ State: _____ Zip: _____

E-mail: _____

I have enclosed $_____ in payment for the checked book(s).

CHECK OUT OUR WEBSITE! www.dorchesterpub.com.
____ Please send me a free catalog.

RAIN VALLEY

LAURAN PAINE

Lauran Paine is one of the West's most powerful storytellers. In the title novella of this collection, Burt Crownover causes quite a stir when he steals into Rain Valley in the middle of the night. It's no surprise the ranchers are suspicious. They've got a herd of highly valuable cattle and any stranger could be a thief. But is Burt a rustler out to con them, or just the man they need to help protect their stock?

Dorchester Publishing Co., Inc.
P.O. Box 6640   5783-2
Wayne, PA 19087-8640 $5.99 US/$7.99 CAN
Please add $2.50 for shipping and handling for the first book and $.75 for each additional book. NY and PA residents, add appropriate sales tax. No cash, stamps, or CODs. Canadian orders require $2.00 for shipping and handling and must be paid in U.S. dollars. Prices and availability subject to change. **Payment must accompany all orders.**

Name: _____

Address: _____

City: _____ State: _____ Zip: _____

E-mail: _____

I have enclosed $_____ in payment for the checked book(s).
CHECK OUT OUR WEBSITE! www.dorchesterpub.com
_____ *Please send me a free catalog.*

ZANE GREY®

CABIN GULCH

In a fit of anger, Joan Randle sends Jim Cleve into the untamed mining camps of Idaho Territory to prove his grit and spirit. Then she regrets their quarrel and sets off after him to bring him back. But she crosses the path of Jack Kells, the notorious mining camp and stagecoach bandit, who captures her and intends to keep her as his woman. He is willing to kill two of his own men to have her all to himself, so how can Joan hope to escape? Her hopes will fade even more when Jim Cleve shows up—and joins Kells' gang....

Dorchester Publishing Co., Inc.
P.O. Box 6640
Wayne, PA 19087-8640

_5826-X
$6.99 US/$8.99 CAN

Please add $2.50 for shipping and handling for the first book and $.75 for each additional book. NY and PA residents, add appropriate sales tax. No cash, stamps, or CODs. Canadian orders require an extra $2.00 for shipping and handling and must be paid in U.S. dollars. Prices and availability subject to change. **Payment must accompany all orders.**

Name: _____

Address: _____

City: _____ State: _____ Zip: _____

E-mail: _____

I have enclosed $_____ in payment for the checked book(s).

CHECK OUT OUR WEBSITE! _www.dorchesterpub.com_
_____ Please send me a free catalog.

ATTENTION
BOOK LOVERS!

CAN'T GET ENOUGH
OF YOUR FAVORITE WESTERNS?

CALL 1-800-481-9191 TO:

- ORDER BOOKS,
- RECEIVE A FREE CATALOG,
- JOIN OUR BOOK CLUBS TO SAVE 30%!

OPEN MON.-FRI. 10 AM-9 PM EST

VISIT
WWW.DORCHESTERPUB.COM
FOR SPECIAL OFFERS AND INSIDE
INFORMATION ON THE AUTHORS
YOU LOVE.

 LEISURE BOOKS
We accept Visa, MasterCard or Discover®.